BIONIC BATS
OF
BAY CITY

Here's what readers from around the country are saying about Johnathan Rand's books:

"MICHIGAN CHILLERS ROCK! My favorite book in the whole world is Mackinaw City Mummies!
                              -Max S., age 8, Michigan

"I finished reading "Dangerous Dolls of Delaware in just three days! It creeped me out!
                              -Brittany K., age 9, Ohio

"My teacher read GHOST IN THE GRAVEYARD to us. I loved it! I can't wait to read GHOST IN THE GRAND!"
                              -Nicholas H., age 8, Arizona

"My brother got in trouble for reading your book after he was supposed to go to bed. He says it's your fault, because your books are so good. But he's not mad at you or anything."
                              -Ariel C., age 10, South Carolina

"Thank you for coming to our school. I thought you would be scary, but you were really funny."
                              -Tyler D., age 10, Michigan

"American Chillers is my favorite series! Can you write them faster so I don't have to wait for the next one? Thank you."
                              -Alex W., age 8, Washington, D.C.

"I can't stop reading AMERICAN CHILLERS! I've read every one twice, and I'm going to read them again!"
                              -Emilee T., age 12, Wisconsin

"Our whole class listened to CREEPY CAMPFIRE CHILLERS with the lights out. It was really spooky!"

-Erin J., age 12, Georgia

"When you write a book about Oklahoma, write it about my city. I've lived here all my life, and it's a freaky place."

-Justin P., age 11, Oklahoma

"When you came to our school, you said that all of your books are true stories. I don't believe you, but I LOVE your books, anyway!"

-Anthony H., age 11, Ohio

"I really liked NEW YORK NINJAS! I'm going to get all of your books!"

-Chandler L., age 10, New York

"Every night I read your books in bed with a flashlight. You write really creepy stories!"

-Skylar P., age 8, Michigan

"My teacher let me borrow INVISIBLE IGUANAS OF ILLINOIS, and I just finished it! It was really, really great!"

-Greg R., age 11, Virginia

"I went to your website and saw your dogs. They are really cute. Why don't you write a book about them?"

-Laura L., age 10, Arkansas

"DANGEROUS DOLLS OF DELAWARE was so scary that I couldn't read it at night. Then I had a bad dream. That book was super-freaky!"

-Sean F., age 9, Delaware

"I have every single book in the CHILLERS series, and I love them!"

-Mike W., age 11, Michigan

"Your books rock!"

-Darrell D ., age 10, Minnesota

"My friend let me borrow one of your books, and now I can't stop! So far, my favorite is WISCONSIN WEREWOLVES. That was a great book!"

-Riley S., age 12, Oregon

"I read your books every single day. They're COOL!"

-Katie M., age 12, Michigan

"I just found out that the #14 book is called CREEPY CONDORS OF CALIFORNIA. That's where I live! I can't wait for this book!"

-Emilio H., age 10, California

"I have every single book that you've written, and I can't decide which one I love the most! Keep writing!"

-Jenna S., age 9, Kentucky

"I love to read your books! My brother does, too!"

-Joey B., age 12, Missouri

"I got IRON INSECTS INVADE INDIANA for my birthday, and it's AWESOME!"

-Colin T., age 10, Indiana

Other books by Johnathan Rand:

Johnathan Rand's
MICHIGAN CHILLERS®

#14:
Bionic Bats
of
Bay City

Johnathan
Rand

An AudioCraft Publishing, Inc. book

This book is a work of fiction. Names, places, characters and incidents are used fictitiously, or are products of the author's very active imagination.

Book storage and warehouses provided by Chillermania!©
Indian River, Michigan

Warehouse security provided by:
Lily Munster and Scooby-Boo

Michigan Chillers #14: Bionic Bats of Bay City
ISBN 13-digit: 978-1-893699-65-5

Librarians/Media Specialists:
PCIP/MARC records available at www.americanchillers.com

Cover illustration by Dwayne Harris
Cover layout and design by Sue Harring

Printed in USA

BIONIC BATS
OF
BAY CITY

VISIT CHILLERMANIA!

WORLD HEADQUARTERS FOR BOOKS BY JOHNATHAN RAND!

CHILLERMANIA!

**I-75 Exit 313
then south
1 mile!**

Visit the HOME for books by Johnathan Rand! Featuring books, hats, shirts, bookmarks and other cool stuff not available anywhere else in the world! Plus, watch the American Chillers website for news of special events and signings at *CHILLERMANIA!* with author Johnathan Rand! Located in northern lower Michigan, on I-75! Take exit 313 . . . then south 1 mile! For more info, call (231) 238-0338. And be afraid! Be veeeery afraaaaaaiiiid . . . .

1

I can remember every single detail about what happened in Bay City that terrible summer. Every thought that flashes through my mind seems like yesterday, and every time I'm reminded of those awful events, a shiver shoots down my spine like a lightning bolt. Sometimes, I even break out in a sweat. I wonder if it will always be this way. I wonder if, years from now, I will still look back on last summer . . . only to cringe with fright.

My sister, Tori, feels the same way. She's eleven—one year younger than I am—and she, too, remembers everything that happened.

But we don't talk about it.

Not anymore.

In fact, Tori refuses to even go out at night anymore, because she's so afraid of what might happen. She's even more freaked out about it than I am.

A few things you should know:

As a twelve year-old boy, I don't get scared easily. Oh, I used to, when I was little. I used to read scary books before I went to bed. When I turned off the light, I would imagine a monster beneath my bed or a creature in my closet. Sometimes, I freaked myself out so badly that I had to sleep with the light on.

But I realized once I grew older that there are no such things as monsters in closets or under beds. And, after a while, I was no longer afraid.

Oh, there are still things that frighten me. For instance, I don't like going down into our basement, because it seems really dark, even with the light on. I imagine creatures hiding behind the

12

furnace or tucked around some of the big storage boxes.

There was one time, however, that I had good reason to be scared. In fact, what happened in the basement one afternoon should have been a warning of things to come.

Mom asked me to go down into the basement, bring up the vacuum, and clean the living room. I wasn't all that happy about it, because I'd planned to meet my friend, Meredith Gaylor, at the school playground. She's been my friend since we were little, and my mom and dad are good friends with her mom and dad. Meredith told me that she'd caught a box turtle by the river, and she'd promised to show it to me. But now I'd have to wait until I finished cleaning the living room.

"Great," I mumbled to myself as I reluctantly opened the basement door.

And that's when I heard a noise.

It was faint—not very loud at all—and it was coming from somewhere in the dark basement.

I should have turned around right there. I should have told my mom about the noise, and then maybe she would have looked into it.

But remember: I don't get scared that easily. After all, I *am* twelve years old. A noise in the basement wasn't about to scare me off. Sure, I was a little leery about going into the basement because it was so dark. But whatever the noise was, I knew that it couldn't be anything that would harm me.

Or could it?

No, I told myself as I took a step down the stairs. *I'm not going to be afraid of anything in the basement. Not today.*

I was about to be proven wrong . . . .

2

I took another step.

Then, I reached out with my left hand and flicked the light switch on the wall. A single bulb at the bottom of the staircase blinked on . . . but there was an immediate *pop!* and the light went out.

"Great," I murmured again.

I turned around.

"Mom!" I shouted, "the light bulb in the basement just burned out!"

"Well, fix it!" came my sister's snappy voice from the living room.

"I can't reach it!" I hollered back.

"Just leave it, Jamie," I heard my mom call out from the kitchen. "Use the flashlight on the shelf. It's right by the door."

Of course. I knew the flashlight was there, because I used it once in a while. Sometimes, when Mom and Dad let us play outside after dark, we'd use the flashlight to play games.

I grabbed the flashlight . . . and that's when I heard the strange squealing noise again, coming from the basement. I stopped for a moment, straining to hear anything more, but the only sounds I heard were from my mom in the kitchen and the television in the living room.

I clicked the light on and aimed it down the steps. Here, it wasn't very dark, but once I reached the basement, I knew I'd need the flashlight to find the vacuum cleaner. Without any lights, our basement is completely dark.

I descended the steps, and the wood boards creaked beneath my feet. When I reached the last step, I stopped. I swept the beam around the room. Shadows moved as the light fell over boxes, an old pool table, a chair with a sheet over it, and a treadmill that had a filmy layer of dust on it. Dad bought the contraption a few years ago, saying that he was going to use it every day. And he did, too—for about a week. Then, he moved it from the living room to the basement, where it still stands to this day. Dad says he's going to pull it out and use it soon, but he's been saying that for months. Mom wants to sell it. Me? I'd like to take it apart. It would be cool to find out how it works.

Sweeping the beam around, I finally found the vacuum cleaner right where it always is: next to my dad's set of golf clubs. They had nearly as much dust on them as the treadmill.

I made my way confidently across the dark basement, following the glowing white beam. I was trying to look on the bright side: it wouldn't take me too long to clean the living room. I would still have time to meet Meredith at the playground and see the box turtle she'd caught.

I was only a few feet from the vacuum cleaner when I heard the squealing again.

This time it was louder, and I knew I was much closer to it. I could also tell that the sound hadn't come from the floor, but from above, up near the ceiling, from a darkened corner of the basement.

I stopped moving and slowly swung the flashlight beam toward the sound. A bright white circle illuminated a shelf that was packed with all kinds of things: coffee cans filled with nails, old books, tools, and my old snowmobile boots that I'd outgrown.

But as I directed the light farther and farther up, I saw something else:

A pair of tiny red eyes, glowing back at me!

3

It took a moment to realize what I was seeing. The two red dots reflected the glare of the flashlight, and I suddenly realized that a pair of eyes was staring back at me.

Slowly, I raised the flashlight beam higher and higher. My heart was racing, and my mind was whirling.

And then, a shadow came into view. The silhouette of a head and ears darkened the wall. The creature squealed again, and I breathed a sigh of relief.

A mouse, I thought. *I can't believe I was startled by a little mouse.*

The tiny creature spun quickly and vanished with a squeal and a flurry of scratching claws. Then, I laughed out loud. It was sort of funny, now that I thought about it.

I picked up the vacuum cleaner, turned, and carried it back to the stairs. Somewhere behind me, the mouse squeaked again, and I shook my head. Mice, like monsters in the closet or under the bed, are nothing to fear.

With the flashlight in one hand and the vacuum in the other, I ascended the stairs. Once again, I could hear Mom fussing in the kitchen, preparing dinner. The television was still on, and I heard Tori laugh at something. She wasn't going to be very happy to see me with the vacuum, because that meant she wouldn't be able to hear the television.

When I reached the last step, I clicked off the flashlight and put it back on the shelf. Then, I stepped into the hall and closed the basement door behind me. I set the vacuum down on the carpeted floor.

"I found a mouse in the basement, Mom," I called out.

"Another one?" Mom replied. "I thought your father had taken care of those things."

"After I finish with the living room, can I go to the school playground?" I asked as I unwound the vacuum cord and plugged it into the wall.

"Not for long," Mom answered. "Dinner will be ready soon."

Hot dog! I thought. After all, I was really looking forward to seeing the box turtle Meredith had caught. I'd never seen one before, except in pictures.

I switched on the vacuum and it whirred to life. Just as I expected, Tori got up from where she was sitting and headed down the hall to her bedroom. Her cat, Merlin, was probably outside. Merlin is all black with white paws. Tori begged Mom and Dad for a cat until she finally got Merlin as a kitten. If that cat is anywhere close when the vacuum starts, he freaks out. He hates the vacuum cleaner.

I got to work. It wouldn't take me more than a few minutes to vacuum the entire living room and pick it up. The sooner I finished, the sooner I could leave . . . unless, of course, Mom wanted me to do something else. She'll do that, once in a while. Just when I think I've finished and can go do what I want, she'll ask me to do something else. It drives me crazy, sometimes.

Sometimes, it's just not fair.

I rushed through the living room with the vacuum, determined to finish as quickly as I could. Actually, it didn't take me long at all. Tori left a pile of her homework on the couch, and after I'd finished vacuuming, I picked it up and carried it to her bedroom door. Then, I knocked twice.

"Your homework is by the door," I said smartly, placing the pile on the floor. "I puked on it."

There was no answer from behind the door, and I grinned. We always tease each other like that. We're not mean to each other, except for once in a while. I think sisters and brothers are just like that sometimes. But we're always kidding around and joking with each other.

I went back to the living room. "All finished, Mom," I said, and I closed my eyes and crossed my fingers, hoping she wouldn't ask me to do anything else.

Mom came into the living room. Her hands were covered with flour, and she was wearing the apron that Tori and I got her for Mother's Day. It's white with red letters that read: KISS THE COOK. She really likes it, and she wears it all the time. What's really funny, though, is that Dad wears it, too. Dad loves to cook, and when he does, he always puts on Mom's apron.

Yeah, I know what you're thinking, and you're right: I have goofy parents. But for the most part, they're okay.

Mom looked around the living room, inspecting my work. "It looks good," she said, to my great relief.

"I'm going to go to the playground for a while," I said.

"Don't be gone long," Mom said, "and be sure to put the vacuum away before you go." Then, she turned and walked back into the kitchen.

Cool, I thought. I was glad I didn't get roped into doing something else . . . like cleaning my room or washing windows.

I grabbed the vacuum cleaner, pushed it down the hall, and stopped at the basement door. Then, I unplugged the electrical cord and wrapped it around the unit. I picked it up by the handle.

I opened the basement door, plucked the flashlight from the shelf, flicked it on, and started down the stairs.

Fearless.

After all: there was no reason to be afraid of anything in the basement. I had a flashlight, so I could see just fine. And I certainly wasn't afraid of a puny little mouse.

Still, I had a strange feeling as I walked down the steps with the flashlight in one hand and the vacuum cleaner in the other. I felt like—

Like I wasn't alone.

No. That's just silly.

Like someone was watching me.

Nope. There was nothing in the basement except a mouse or two and a bunch of clutter—I was certain.

But I was wrong.

Something else was down there, waiting in the shadows, watching warily as I descended farther and farther into the basement, deeper into the darkness.

I should have listened to that little voice in my head that told me something wasn't right . . . but I didn't. I just kept going down the steps.

Soon, however, I would realize:

There was something down there.

Something was waiting for me in the darkness—and that something was only a few feet away . . . .

4

Have you ever had a feeling that something wasn't right? That something really bad was about to happen?

I have. Not often, but it's always a weird feeling. It usually starts at the back of my neck and goes up into my head. My hair feels all tingly, like it's going to stand straight up. Sometimes, I get a really strange chill.

Then, the feeling starts creeping down my spine. Sometimes, a shiver will race through me. Almost always, the feeling causes me to freeze.

Like now.

I stopped at the bottom of the stairs. The feeling of terror was so strong that I almost dropped the flashlight and the vacuum . . . but I didn't. Although I was suddenly very frightened, I stood my ground, nervously sweeping the flashlight beam back and forth.

What are you afraid of, Jamie? I wondered, and I began to think my imagination was getting the best of me. *There's nothing to be afraid of down here.*

The beam of light splashed across Dad's old treadmill. Shadows swayed and fled, and I kept moving the beam around the basement. Finally, when the feeling of terror faded, I started across the floor. I moved slowly because I was still a little nervous, but I kept telling myself not to be afraid.

I shined the flashlight up, illuminating the shelf where I'd seen the mouse. He was gone, of course, but the beam also lit up a small cardboard box next to it, and my train of thought changed.

Box, I thought. *Box turtle. Meredith caught a box turtle, and she's bringing it to the school playground so I can see it.*

That made me move a little quicker. After all, I *was* anxious to see the turtle.

Reaching the other side of the basement, I returned the vacuum to its proper place, turned—

And heard a noise.

It was a squeak . . . of sorts. Not at all the squeak that a mouse would make, but a different sound altogether.

Another heavy feeling of horror crept over me. It felt like a million tiny spiders were crawling all over my skin as I slowly swung the flashlight around the room.

"Who's there?" I asked, and my voice trembled. Then, I realized how silly it was. There was no one in the basement except me. Mom was upstairs in the kitchen, and Tori was in her bedroom. Whatever had made the noise wasn't *human.* Of course, that thought didn't make me feel any better.

But I stood my ground, slowly moving the flashlight beam around the dark basement. I wished the light bulb hadn't burned out! Then, it wouldn't be so dark.

Not seeing the source of the noise, I began walking toward the basement steps. The only sound was the soft scuffing of my feet against the cement floor.

When I reached the stairs, I placed my foot on the first step. I felt better, because light poured down from the open door above.

Suddenly, there was a noise from behind me . . . and something sharp dug into my neck!

5

I was so scared I dropped the flashlight. It landed on my left foot . . . which would have hurt a lot, had I noticed it. Right now, I was too freaked out by what was biting my neck!

My heart went into overdrive, thrashing madly in my chest. I whirled around, accidentally kicking the flashlight across the floor. It skidded noisily, making metallic cracks and bangs, until it hit something and stopped. The light instantly went out.

In the same instant, I raised my hands up to pry away whatever was at my neck . . . and found something soft and warm, something that felt like—

Skin?

Then, I saw an arm.

My *sister's* arm.

She had been waiting in a broom closet at the bottom of the steps, and had reached out and poked my neck!

"You!" I snapped. "I should've known!"

"That was funny!" Tori said, pulling her arm away. She was laughing, and I felt pretty silly. And, I admit, I was a little mad. Tori sure had scared me.

"What did you poke me with?!?!" I demanded.

Tori shook her head. "Nothing," she replied, really innocent-like. "Just my nails."

She held up her hand, displaying her fingers. Her nails are only a little longer than mine, but they sure felt sharp when she had pressed them against my neck.

And I made a decision right then and there to get even with her. Oh, I wasn't sure what I was going to do, but I'd figure out something. Maybe I would hide in her closet and wait for her to climb into bed. Then, I could jump out and roar like a monster! That would freak her out, for sure! I'd probably get into trouble, but it would be worth it.

"How did you get down here, anyway?" I asked. I was beginning to calm down, and my heart wasn't pounding so heavily anymore.

"While you were vacuuming," Tori replied as she climbed out of the closet. "I closed my bedroom door so you would think I was there. But I knew you'd be coming down to the basement to put the vacuum cleaner away."

"I'll get you back," I said. "Just you wait."

Tori slipped out of the closet, and the door made a squeaking sound. That's what I had heard a few moments before: the squeak from the closet door. It must've moved while Tori was hiding, waiting for me.

She squeezed past me and bounded up the steps. "Good luck trying to get me back," she said, and she reached the top of the stairs, bolted out the open basement door, and vanished.

"I will," I said quietly to myself. "I'll get her back, if it's the last thing I do."

In the dim light coming from the top of the stairs, I could see the flashlight on the floor. It lay near the bottom of a metal shelf.

Great, I thought. *It's probably broken.* Well, at least it wasn't all my fault. If I got into trouble for breaking it, Tori would be in trouble, too. After all: she was the one who frightened me. If it hadn't been for her, I wouldn't have dropped it in the first place.

I walked to the flashlight and picked it up. Turns out it wasn't broken, after all. The battery cover had come loose, and when I snapped it back into place, the light came on.

I hurried to the stairs, bounding up two at a time. Then, I put the flashlight back on the shelf and closed the door behind me.

"I'm going to the school playground, Mom," I said as I hustled down the hall.

"Remember what I said," Mom replied from the kitchen. "Don't be gone long. Dinner will be ready in half an hour."

"I'll be back," I said, and I opened the front door and bolted outside, not knowing that danger lurked in the sky, only moments away . . . .

6

I bounded off the porch and landed in the soft grass. Around me, the familiar sights and sounds of Bay City replaced the staleness of our house. Oh, it's not that I don't like our house, it's just that I'd rather be outdoors than inside. Some of my friends think that's weird. They'd rather be inside, playing video games or on the computer. Not me. I like to be outside, even in the winter. Bay City can get some pretty fierce snowstorms, too . . . which can be a lot of fun.

But not now. It was summer. July 10th, to be exact, and the days were hot and steamy.

Meredith and I, along with Alec Germain, a new kid who lives a few blocks away, had been spending a lot of time outdoors. The neighborhood where we live has a lot of big, old homes with big yards and huge trees. And there are a lot of kids my age, which is cool.

Bay City is located near the mid-portion of the state of Michigan, close to Lake Huron, one of Michigan's five Great Lakes. In fact, it's one of the busiest shipping ports in the state. You can see huge freighters pass by in the Saginaw River, which isn't far from our house. There are lots of cool places to play along the riverbanks, too. In fact, that's where Meredith said she'd found the box turtle.

I sprinted across the lawn and raced down the sidewalk. There were a lot of cars passing by on the street, which is pretty typical. I could hear the thumping of music, engines idling, and a few honks in the distance. Several pigeons waddled on the sidewalk ahead of me, and they took off in a flurry of flapping wings as I approached.

In a few minutes, I had reached the school playground. It's sort of a hang out for those of us who attend school there, but I didn't see anyone around tonight. Not even Meredith . . . which was a little strange. She's usually always at the playground before I get there.

I decided I'd sit on a swing and wait for her. I knew she wouldn't be long. And I didn't mind waiting, either. I was already starting to think of ways I could get back at my sister for scaring me in the basement.

I didn't have long to wait. I heard a shout in the distance and recognized it as Meredith's voice right away.

But—

She sounded *panicked.*

"Jamie!" she shouted, and I snapped my head around. On the other side of the playground, she was running, carrying a brown box. And even though she was far away, I could see that she was freaked out about something.

"*Watch out!*" she shrieked. "*They're in the sky! Watch out!*"

I looked up . . . just in time to see a dark shape swooping down on me!

7

In the next instant, I dropped to the ground and covered my head with my hands. Although I didn't get a good look at what was attacking me, I wasn't taking any chances.

"Are you all right?!?!" I heard Meredith shout. I raised my head a little and saw her blond hair bobbing as she ran. She was still carrying the box in front of her, and she still had a very worried look on her face.

I turned my head farther and looked up. I couldn't see anything except for trees and blue sky. The late afternoon sun was bleeding through tree limbs, and I squinted and shaded my eyes with my right hand. But I didn't see anything more.

"I'm fine," I said, scrambling to my knees. I looked up to the sky, then to Meredith. She had stopped running and was now hurrying toward me at a fast walk, carrying the box with both hands.

"Did he bite you?" Meredith asked as she drew near. She stared at my neck, probably expecting to see a wound.

"I don't even know what it was," I replied, getting to my feet. Sand and small twigs stuck to my jeans and T-shirt, and I brushed them off.

"It was a bat!" Meredith exclaimed, glancing nervously into the air. "It was the biggest bat I've ever seen! He was black and hairy and had fangs. Didn't you see it?"

"No, I guess I didn't," I replied, looking into the sky. "I saw a dark shadow, but that was it."

"It was a bat, and it was ginormous!" Meredith gasped. That's a word she made up: ginormous. She says it's a cross between 'gigantic' and 'enormous'. It's not a real word, but she uses it a lot when she's describing something really big.

I shook my head. "I saw *something*," I said. "But I couldn't tell what it was."

"You're lucky," Meredith said. "If he would have bitten you, you would've been in a lot of trouble. He would have sucked all of your blood! That's what bats do, you know."

I rolled my eyes. "Bats don't suck your blood, Meredith," I said. "They eat bugs, and they usually leave people alone. In fact, they don't even like coming out in the daylight. Are you sure it was a bat?"

Meredith bobbed her head. "I'm sure it was. I saw it a few minutes ago, and it came after me. That's why I ran off." She pointed. "It chased me across the playground. I came back because I knew you'd be here, and I wanted to warn you."

"Well, whatever it was," I said, "it's gone now. Are you sure it wasn't a pigeon or a blackbird?"

"I know a bat when I see one," Meredith insisted. "And *that* was a bat. A ginormous one!"

"Okay, okay, I believe you," I said. "But he's gone now. We'll probably never see him again."

Oh, we'd see him again, all right . . . a lot sooner than I could have ever imagined!

8

Meredith knelt down and placed the box on the ground. There was a lid on it, and she carefully lifted it off. Inside was the box turtle she'd caught.

"This is Clyde," Meredith said as she lifted the turtle from the box.

"You named him 'Clyde'?" I snickered.

"What's wrong with 'Clyde'?" she demanded.

"Nothing," I replied, shaking my head. "It just seems like an odd name for a turtle."

"I caught him," Meredith said, "so I can call him anything I want. Besides . . . I'm only keeping him for a couple more days. Then, I'm going to let him go where I found him, down by the river."

The box turtle was really cool. His shell was shaped like a helmet, and he was black with yellow splotches and bars. His legs, head, and tail had the same markings. I'd never seen a box turtle before, and he really looked cool. He was quite a bit different from the painted turtles and the snappers that I've seen in and around the river.

We watched him crawl around on the ground for a few minutes. Like most turtles, he couldn't move very fast on land. But in the water, I was sure he was a lot faster. I've tried to catch turtles in the water before, and sometimes they're so quick that they can get away before I even get close.

Finally, Meredith picked up Clyde and put him back in the box. "I keep him in a big wood box my dad gave me," she said. "He has his own pool that I made from an old skillet."

"That's cool," I said. "I wish my parents would let me keep a turtle . . . even if it was just for a few days."

Suddenly, we heard a shout in the distance.

"Hey, guys!"

I recognized the voice instantly. As we turned, we saw Alec Germain coming our way on a skateboard, zipping across the empty school parking lot. When he reached the edge of the pavement, he leapt off, snapped up the skateboard, and tucked it under his arm as he trotted across the playground toward us. Alec and his family moved here from Detroit a few months ago, and he's really great. He's the same height that I am, and he has brown hair like me . . . only his is a bit longer.

"Hey, guys," he repeated as he stopped.

"Hi, Alec," Meredith said.

"How's it going?" I asked.

"Great, now," he said. "Man! I sure ran into some kooky people on the way over here."

"What do you mean?" I asked.

Alec hiked his thumb over his shoulder. "Back there, downtown. There were a bunch of people running all over the place, screaming something about giant bats. Can you believe that?"

Meredith and I looked at each other with frozen expressions. Then, we looked back at Alec.

"Really?" Meredith asked. "Did you see any?"

"Are you kidding?" Alec said. "Giant bats? I think those people themselves were batty."

I was going to tell Alec that I had seen a giant bat, too . . . but I hadn't. Oh, *something* had swooped down at me, but I didn't actually *see* what it was. Meredith saw something, though, and she was certain it was a bat.

But she didn't say anything to Alec. She probably figured that he would think she was batty, too.

"Well," Meredith said, picking up the box and getting to her feet. "I've got to get going. I'll see you guys tomorrow."

"See ya," I replied, and Meredith turned and walked away.

"Hey," Alec said. "We're getting some people together for a game of hide-and-seek after dark. You wanna play?"

"Yeah!" I said. That was something we did a lot during the summer. Playing hide-and-seek after dark was a blast. It was scary, sometimes, because if you were 'it', it meant you had to search dark shadows around the neighborhood. But it was always a lot of fun . . . especially if a lot of kids played.

But tonight would be different.

Tonight wasn't going to be fun.

Tonight, after dark, horrible things were going to happen, and I would soon be wishing that I'd never decided to play hide-and-seek . . . .

9

We hiked across the playground, over the parking lot, and through downtown. Alec carried his skateboard, and we talked while we walked.

"You should have seen them," he said.

"Seen who?" I asked.

"Those people," he replied. "They were running all over the place, trying to hide. Some little kid was crying, saying that a giant bat had attacked him."

"You know," I said, "Meredith said she saw something like a giant bat. She said it was ginormous."

"What's 'ginormous'?" Alec asked curiously.

"Oh, it's a word she made up," I answered. "It means that it was really big."

"There's no such thing as giant bats," Alec said. Then, he thought about it for a moment. "Well, not around here, there's not," he continued. "In other countries, bats can get big. But I've never heard of a bat, anywhere, bigger than a robin or a blue jay. The only bats we have in Michigan are brown bats. They don't get much bigger than a sparrow and can eat five thousand bugs in one night."

"How come you know so much about bats?" I asked.

Alec stopped walking. "At my old school, I did a report about bats," he said. "I had to stand up in front of the class and everything, for five minutes, and tell everyone about them. So, I did a lot of studying."

"Were you nervous?" I asked.

Alec looked at me, puzzled. "No," he said. "I study all the time."

"No," I said. "I meant standing up in front of everyone."

"Oh, I was a little nervous about *that,*" Alec replied. "But it wasn't too bad."

We started walking again, and I glanced up at the sky. A few pigeons flew beneath white, puffy clouds, and a crow was being chased by several smaller birds.

But there were no bats.

"Well, those people must've seen *something,*" I said.

"Probably just seagulls," Alec said.

"Yeah, probably," I said.

We rounded a corner onto my block. "I've got to go eat," I said. "I'll see you later tonight, just before dark."

"We'll all meet at my house," Alec said.

"Got it," I replied. "See you later."

Alec walked away, and I turned and continued in the opposite direction. I could see my house in the distance . . . but I could also see something else: a dark shadow on the ground, moving quickly across the street, right above my head.

All too late, I realized that the shadow wasn't headed across the street . . . it was headed toward me! I tried to duck and raise my arm to block whatever it was, but it was too late. I felt a sharp pain at the back of my neck, and I was sent tumbling to the pavement!

10

Fortunately, I was able to break my fall with my hands. My palms stung as they hit the pavement, but the fall could have been a lot worse. I could have easily broken a bone.

At that moment, however, I wasn't all that concerned about falling . . . I was more concerned with what had attacked me from the sky!

I rolled to my side, off the sidewalk, and into the grass . . . and quickly discovered what had attacked me.

A kite!

That's right . . . a paper kite that was about three feet tall and two feet wide. It was striped with all sorts of colors: red, green, blue, yellow, orange, purple, and more, and it had a tail made of short cloths that had been tied together. There was a string tied to it, but it was only a few feet long. It must have broken while someone was flying it, and it came down . . . right on *me!*

I got to my feet and heard a distant shout.

"There it is! Over there!"

I turned to see another friend, Bobby Reese, running toward me. Bobby is my age, and we're in the same grade at school. In fact, last year, we were in the same class.

I picked up the kite and held it up. "Looking for something?!?!" I shouted.

"Yeah!" Bobby exclaimed as he approached. He slowed and stopped on the sidewalk in front of me, huffing and puffing. "Man! I thought it was gone for good!" He turned and pointed. "The string broke way back there, two blocks over! I've been trying to catch up with it, but the wind kept taking it farther and farther away!"

I handed the kite to Bobby. "Here you go," I said. "I don't think it's broken or anything."

"Thanks," Bobby said. He took the kite and inspected it. "I just got it yesterday. I would hate to lose it."

"Hey," I said, "a bunch of us are getting together tonight to play hide-and-seek. You wanna come?"

Bobby's eyes lit up. "Yeah!" he exclaimed. "That would be a ton of fun!"

"We're all going to meet at Alec's house just before dark," I said.

"I'll be there!" Bobby said. He seemed really excited. If we could get a bunch of us together to play hide-and-seek, we'd all have a great time.

Of course, if we knew then what we know now, none of us would have set foot out of our homes after dark.

But you can't always know what lies in the future . . . and our future was going to be nothing less than a night of horror!

11

After dinner, Mom had a list of things for me to do around the house. I had to clean my room, which wasn't so bad. I keep it pretty clean most of the time. Tori is the one with the messy room. She has clothes all over the place, and Mom is constantly after her to put things away and take care of her stuff.

After I cleaned my room, I mowed the lawn. That took almost an hour, because I had to mow both the front and the back. Plus, the lawnmower blade was getting dull and wasn't cutting the grass very well. Plus, the bag had a hole in it, which meant that I had to go back over the yard with a rake and put the grass into garbage bags. It's not a lot of fun. I complain to Mom and Dad that they never make Tori mow the lawn . . . but they say she's too young. I started mowing the lawn when I was eleven, so why couldn't Tori? Sheesh.

Finally, I got everything done, which was a good thing: it was nearing dark. I knew that some of my friends were probably already arriving at Alec's house. I put the lawnmower in the garage, ran around the front of our house, and opened the door.

"Mom!" I shouted. "I'm going to go to Alec's to play hide-and-seek!"

"Me too! Me too!" Tori shouted from the living room.

"You weren't invited," I said.

"But I want to play, too!" Tori insisted, leaping off the couch and coming to the front door.

"Let your sister go along and play," Mom said.

Rats.

Don't get me wrong: I like my sister. But she always wants to tag along everywhere I go. She can be really annoying, sometimes.

Then, I had an idea.

Hey, I thought, *tonight might be the night I can get her back for scaring me this morning!*

"Okay, Tori," I said. "You can come along and play."

"Goody!" Tori giggled, and she pushed past me and bounded off the porch and into the front yard. I pulled the front door closed and joined her.

"We'll have to be careful tonight," I said as we made our way to the sidewalk. On the other side of the road, one of the streetlights turned on. It wouldn't be long before it was dark.

"Why?" Tori asked.

"Haven't you heard?" I asked.

"About what?" Tori said.

"About the giant bats," I said. I made sure that I sounded really worried, and I looked up into the darkening sky, as if I might see one swooping down at that very moment.

Tori stopped walking and looked at me. I could tell that she didn't know whether to believe me or not. I stopped a few feet away and turned to look at her.

"Oh, I know what you're thinking," I continued, "but lots of people have seen them. In fact, several people have been bitten already."

Tori looked nervously up into the sky.

"I'm not making it up," I said, and we started walking again.

"Really?" she asked.

Yes! I thought. *She's believing me!*

"Yep," I said, glancing into the sky again. "We'll all have to be careful tonight."

At the time, I thought it was funny. I had Tori falling for my story hook, line, and sinker.

Trouble was: I didn't know how right I was. There really *were* giant bats in Bay City.

In fact, some were watching us at that very moment . . . .

12

Before we reached Alec's house, we could already hear laughter and shouting. Kids were already arriving, and I knew we were in for a fun time. The night was warm and clear. As it grew darker, I could see stars appearing.

"Looks like we'll have a lot of kids playing tonight," I said to Tori as we hurried along the sidewalk.

"I've never played before," Tori said.

"Yes, you have," I replied.

"Oh, I've played hide-and-seek before," Tori said. "But not with your friends."

"It's not anything different," I said. "All you have to do is find a place to hide and stay there. And there are lots of great places to hide on Alec's block . . . especially after dark. That is, of course, if we don't get attacked by giant bats."

Tori looked into the sky. "I wonder where they came from?" she said.

This is too funny! I thought. *My sister actually believes there are giant bats in Bay City!*

"I don't know where they came from," I said, "but I hope I don't get bit. I hear that their fangs are five inches long."

"That would really hurt," Tori said.

"I hear they can even carry people away," I said, laying it on thicker and thicker.

Tori's jaw dropped. "That's horrible!" she said, still looking nervously into the sky as we walked. "Maybe we shouldn't be outdoors."

"We should be careful," I said. "I think Mom and Dad would be mad if we got bit."

I smiled. I couldn't believe Tori was falling for it, and I started thinking about more things I could do to really freak her out.

It was then that I stopped. I opened my mouth and froze on the sidewalk. My arm shot out, and I pointed to something in the dark shadows between two houses.

"Look out!" I shrieked. *"There's a giant bat right there! He's flying right at us!"*

13

I took off running. Tori screamed, and she, too, began to run. I was having a hard time, because I wanted to burst out laughing! I hadn't seen a bat—I was only kidding! And Tori believed me!

Yes, I know . . . it probably wasn't a nice thing to do to my sister. But remember: she was the one who'd hid in the basement closet and scared me. I was only getting back at her for what she did.

I ran until I reached Alec's house. Meredith was there, and so was Bobby, along with a few other neighborhood kids. It was still a little light out, but all of the streetlights were on. The sky was a purple-gray color. Soon, the neighborhood would be cloaked by the night.

I slowed to a walk and finally burst out laughing. Tori was still shrieking as she came up behind me, and all the kids stopped what they were doing and looked at us.

Tori must've suddenly figured out that I was only teasing her, because she looked angry.

"You fibber!" she said.

I was still laughing. "I told her that a giant bat was attacking us!" I explained to everyone. "She believed me!"

"That wasn't nice!" Tori fumed.

"Hey, I was just getting you back from this morning," I said. "You hid in the basement closet and scared me. Now we're even."

Tori still looked mad, but she didn't say anything else. I think she realized that she deserved what she got.

"I heard that some people said they saw giant bats today," Bobby said, nodding his head. A few other kids nodded along with him. Even Meredith nodded her head. After all, she saw one, too. But we didn't talk much more about it. After all, there were no such things as giant bats.

We all talked and chatted while we waited for it to get dark. I talked to a few kids I knew from school, but mostly, I talked with Alec, Meredith, and Bobby. Tori didn't say much of anything. I think she was still mad at me for teasing her about the bat.

Finally, when the sky had grown black, when billions of stars twinkled and we could see a quarter moon rising, we decided it was dark enough to play hide-and-seek.

"I'll be 'it' first," a kid said. It was Andrew Davies, I think. He was two grades ahead of me, and I didn't know him very well.

"Okay," Alec said, and we all started to scatter. I hadn't counted, but I think there were about twelve of us who were playing.

"I'm going to count to thirty, then I'm coming to find you," Andrew said loudly as he walked to the porch and sat. He covered his eyes and started counting.

It was a pretty simple game, really. All we would do was find a good place to hide before Andrew counted to thirty. If he found us, or if we didn't find a place to hide, he would chase after us and try to tag us. If someone made it back to the porch before he found him or her or before he tagged him or her, that person was 'safe' . . . and that meant that kid wouldn't be 'it' during the next round. Even though it's a really simple game to play, it's always a lot of fun—especially after dark.

I headed across the street and darted between two houses. There were a bunch of bushes behind one of the houses, and I knew I could hide there without being seen. Of course, we'd all played hide-and-seek so much that most of us knew all of the good places to hide. The trick was finding a place where you could see the porch . . . and the person who was 'it'.

I snuggled into the bushes and pulled a few branches away so I could see across the street.

Andrew was still counting loudly, and his voice echoed up and down the block.

"Twenty two . . . twenty-three . . . twenty-four—"

With any luck, he would search the other side of the street first. If that happened, then I might have time to sprint across the street and make it to the porch. Then, I wouldn't be 'it' on the next round.

"—Twenty-five . . . ."

I heard a noise above me. It was a soft, scuffing sound, like leather rubbing against metal.

"—Twenty-six . . . ."

At first, I ignored the sound. It wasn't very loud, and I wasn't the least bit worried . . . or interested. The only thing I was interested in was Andrew across the street. He was almost done counting.

"—Twenty-seven . . . ."

Then, I heard more shuffling. Louder.

"—Twenty-eight . . . ."

I looked up.

I saw a dark shadow, clinging to the eave beneath the roof. The shadow was as big as I was.

"—Twenty-nine . . . ."

Then, it spread its wings.

"—Thirty! Ready or not, here I come!" Andrew shouted from the porch.

I forgot all about our game of hide-and-seek. I forgot to watch Andrew to see where he was going.

I forgot about everything. The only thing that had my attention was the enormous creature above me. It opened its mouth and let out a horrible, awful screech. Two long fangs glared in the pale glow of the streetlight. Its wings spread wide, and the horrible beast took flight.

Problem was, he was flying directly at me!

14

As you can imagine, I didn't just scream . . . I howled my head off! I was tangled in the bushes, and it was difficult to move.

But, as it turned out, being tucked in the branches probably saved my life. The creature swooped down, narrowly missing the top of the bushes. It squealed again, turned up, and flew off into the night.

I stayed where I was for a moment, too frightened to move or do anything. I was hoping that it was gone, but I couldn't be sure.

Meredith was right, after all! I thought, trying hard to calm my raging heart. *She really* had *seen a giant bat!*

And I was certain that was what the creature was. I'd seen enough bats to know what they look like . . . but I certainly had never seen one that big before!

"Over that way!" someone shouted from down the street. "I think it came from over there!"

I scrambled out of the bushes, stood, and glanced warily into the night sky. I saw millions of stars and the thumbnail-shaped moon . . . but there was no sign of any bat.

"He sounded hurt!" someone else shouted, and soon, everyone was gathered around me, panting for breath.

"Was that you who screamed?" Alec asked.

"Yeah!" I said. "You're not going to believe me, but I just saw a gigantic bat!"

"You're right," Bobby said. "We don't believe you. Why did you holler like that?"

"Because I really *did* see a giant bat!" I exclaimed, turning and pointing at the roof of the house. "He was up there, hanging against the wall, up near the roof. He attacked me!"

Tori looked at me and frowned. "He's making it up!" she said. "He said the same thing to me on the way here, and I got scared."

"Guys," I said, "I swear! I really saw a giant bat! He was as big as me!"

Meredith spoke. "I think he's telling the truth," she said. "I saw a huge bat earlier today. It was ginormous."

"And there were people in the city that said they saw giant bats," Alec said. "I thought they were nuts."

We all looked up into the sky, but there wasn't anything to see except stars and the moon. Crickets chirped, and the streetlights gave off an electric buzzing sound. In a house nearby, I could hear a television set blaring.

"Well, I think he's making it up," Bobby said.

"But what if he's not?" Andrew asked. "If there really are giant bats flying around, we should probably tell someone. And we probably shouldn't be outside after dark."

"I say we all go home," Meredith said. "I'm getting freaked out. I don't want to get attacked by a ginormous bat."

"Hey, anyone who's a scaredy-cat can go home if they want," some kid said. "We can all go finish our game over at my house. Anybody with me?"

Slowly, kids began shuffling off. Soon, there were only five of us: Tori, Meredith, Alec, Bobby, and me.

"Why didn't you go with them?" I asked Bobby. "I didn't think you believed me."

"I'm not sure what to believe," Bobby said. "But I know strange things can happen. I heard once about some crazy carnival or something in Kalamazoo where some weirdo clowns locked everyone inside the festival grounds. That's hard to believe, but it happened."

"Well, I'm going to go home and tell my mom and dad," I said. "They'll know what to do. They might even call the police."

As it turned out, though, none of us would be going home.

Not at that moment, anyway.

Maybe not forever.

Once again, I had that really weird feeling come over me, like I'd had earlier in the day in the basement. A thin band of electricity was humming up and down my spine. I think everyone else felt something, too, because we all stopped talking.

A movement above caught my eye, and I looked up. So did Meredith, Alec, Bobby, and Tori.

Suddenly, Meredith pointed. "There!" she shouted. "There's something moving right there!"

She was right!

We could definitely see a dark silhouette in the sky . . . and then we saw something else.

Another one.

And another.

Two more.

They were above us, circling over the treetops, wings flapping, bodies whirling.

Then, as if one of them had given the others a signal, the cloud of bats descended upon us!

15

I'll tell you one thing: you've never seen five kids run so fast in your entire life! If anyone was watching us, they probably thought we were running a marathon race!

The bats seemed to swarm all around us. They were huge—much bigger than any flying creature I'd ever seen before—and their heads were as big as basketballs! They squealed as they flew, and I just knew that at any second I was going to feel the sharp pain of razor-sharp teeth biting into me.

Meredith was screaming, and so was Tori. We tried to run to Alec's house to get inside, but the bats just circled in front of us and blocked our path, and we had to run down the street. We knew it would only be a matter of moments before people heard us screaming and would come to help. What they would do, I didn't know. In fact, they might not be able to do anything at all.

That really scared me. A thousand thoughts banged around in my brain. *Where did the bats come from? Why are they after us? Bats are supposed to eat bugs, not humans!*

None of those thoughts mattered, though. Right now, I was too worried about a bat getting me. Even as I ran, I could see their horrible eyes glaring at me. I have never, ever been so terrified.

"We've got to get indoors!" I shrieked. *"It's the only way we'll be able to get away from them!"*

"But they're all around us!" Tori screeched.

However, as we ran, I noticed that there weren't as many bats after us. I could see them farther away, swooping low beneath streetlights before arcing up and vanishing, blending into the night sky.

We ran three blocks, where there is a city park with a baseball field. "Let's hide in a dugout!" Alec said. "That way, we'll at least have a wall and a roof over our head to help protect us!"

The five of us sprinted across the ball field. It was really dark and I nearly tripped, but we all made it. I could still hear the heavy whooshing of wings flapping. I knew that there were still bats after us, but there didn't seem to be as many of them.

The five of us dove into the dugout. I tripped on a bench and fell into the back wall. My shoulder hit something so hard that I heard a snap, and I thought I'd broken a bone. Turns out, it was only the wood cracking. But it hurt, anyway.

And the bats were still around. We couldn't see them very well, because it was a lot darker here at the ball field than it was near Alec's house. Here, there were no streetlights to illuminate the field or the bats. But we could see their huge, dark shapes as they swooped down and up, again and again.

They weren't going to give up or go away, that was for sure.

I scrambled to my feet, but had to duck down quickly to get away from a bat that was coming for me. Again, I tripped over a bench. There were a bunch of them in the dugout. When teams played, they took the extra benches and lined them up around the field for spectators.

It was the benches that probably saved our lives . . . at least at that moment.

"Let's use the benches to build a wall!" Bobby shouted. In the darkness, I watched his shape bend over, grab a bench, and stand it on its end. They aren't very big—maybe six feet long—but they're heavy. I helped Bobby with the bench, and we leaned it up to begin building a wall around the open parts of the dugout. Meredith and Tori worked together, and Alec helped Bobby and me.

It took a few minutes, but we succeeded in barricading the dugout, creating a solid wall all around it. The bats were still trying to get at us, but the benches kept them out.

We knew we were safe—for now.

What we didn't know was that we were in for a long, long night of terror.

16

We waited in silence. After a few minutes, we could no longer hear the flapping of wings or the angry squealing of the bats. In fact, we couldn't hear much of anything, except some traffic in the distance. There were no crickets to be heard, no other night sounds at all.

"I feel like I'm going to wake up at any moment," Meredith whispered, "and this will all have been just a bad nightmare."

"Wishful thinking," I said. "If it's a nightmare, it's happening to all of us at the same time."

"Where did those things come from?" Tori asked. Her voice trembled, and I knew she was really scared. I couldn't blame her. I was scared, too.

"I don't know and I don't care," Bobby said. "I hope we don't see any more of those fangy-freaks for as long as I live."

Somewhere in the city, a police siren wailed.

Then another.

And another.

Soon the night was filled with various screaming sirens, warbling at different pitches and volumes.

"Someone else must've seen the bats," I said, "and they called the police."

"But what are they going to do about them?" Meredith asked. "Are they going to try and catch them?"

"Let's not worry about that right now," I said. "Let's just worry about getting out of this alive."

"I'll bet my parents are freaking out right now," Alec said.

He was sure right about that. *All* of our parents would be freaking out. Once they found out that there were giant bats attacking the city and we hadn't come home . . . well, they'd be going crazy. I felt bad, because I knew that they would be really worried. I tried to think of ways we could let them know, but I couldn't come up with anything.

"How long are we going to wait here?" Tori asked.

"As long as it takes," Alec replied. "Until we know it's safe."

"But the longer we wait, the more our parents are going to freak out," I said. "Besides . . . maybe the bats are gone. Maybe they flew off to somewhere else."

"Maybe," Bobby said, "but do we really want to take that chance?"

"We made it here from Alec's house in less than a minute," I said. "Think about it: if we ran fast, we could be safe inside his house in less than sixty seconds. Then, we could all call our parents and let them know that we're okay."

No one said anything. I could tell they were thinking my idea over. Sure, it might be risky, but what if the bats were gone? Then, we wouldn't be in any danger at all.

Finally, Bobby spoke. "I'm with Jamie," he said. "I know that my parents are probably worried sick about me. I've got to let them know that I'm all right."

"Me, too, I guess," Meredith said.

"Count me in," Tori said. "I say we make a run for it."

Alec finally agreed. "All right," he said, "but I hope we're right. I hope those bats are gone."

We could still hear sirens throughout the city. Every so often, we could hear someone shouting, but they were a long way away. I'd hoped that a police car would have driven by the field, but no cars passed by at all.

"Here's what we'll do," Alec said, and we began to make a plan . . . a plan that was about to fail.

We just didn't know it yet.

On any other day, our plan would have been simple: all we would do was run from the dugout, across the ball field, and down the street. Then, we would run into Alec's house, and we'd be safe.

We stood in the dugout for a long time, just making sure no bats were around. We could still hear sirens around the city and some very distant shouting.

But there was no sign of any bats. The only things we saw in the sky were stars and the moon.

"Jamie, help me move this bench," Alec said. Together, we pulled down one of the benches that had helped create our barricade and laid it on the ground.

"Do you see anything?" Meredith asked.

"It's too dark," I replied. "But I don't see anything in the sky."

We stood in silence for nearly a minute. I think we were all a little scared. When we began our run to Alec's house, we would be out in the open. If there were any bats flying around, they would be able to see us.

"If bats are blind, how will they know where we are?" my sister asked.

"Bats aren't blind," Alec replied. "That's just an old wives' tale. Bats can see fine, but lots of them use echolocation to hunt for bugs."

Tori was puzzled. "What in the world is echo . . . echolo . . . echo—"

"Echolocation," Alec repeated. "Some bats can bounce sounds off things and sort of 'see' from the echo that's created."

"How do you know so much about bats?" Bobby asked.

"Like I told Jamie earlier today: I did an oral report on bats for school. And I got an A on it, too."

"But that means that the bats will be able to detect our movement, even if they don't see us," Meredith said.

"True," Alec replied. "We're just going to have to be fast. Everybody ready?"

I didn't know if I was ready or not. I tried to keep thinking that as soon as we started to run, we'd be safe in Alec's home in less than a minute. Then, I'd be able to call Mom and Dad and let them know Tori and I were all right.

"Let's get this over with," Bobby said.

Alec was the first to leave the dugout, and he stood just outside, in the open.

"I think it's all clear," he whispered. *"Everyone come out, and we'll run together as a group."*

I stepped between the benches and stood next to Alec. Bobby followed, then Meredith, then Tori.

"I hope we're doing the right thing," Tori said.

"We'll be safe inside my house in no time," Alec said. "Everyone ready?"

We were.

"We'll go on the count of three," Alec said. "One . . . two . . . *three!*"

We took off running across the baseball field. It's too bad we weren't playing an actual game of baseball and rounding the bases, because we were all running like gazelles. I can run pretty fast, but I stayed behind in our group, so that if something happened to Tori, I could help her.

Turns out, Tori wouldn't be the one needing help.

It was Meredith.

There was no warning, no sounds, nothing. One moment we were running along at breakneck speed across the ball field. The next moment, a huge, dark form swooped up from behind, barely missing my head. I didn't even have time to shout as the bat spun forward, sunk his teeth into Meredith's neck . . . and lifted her clear off the ground!

18

Meredith screamed as the giant bat attacked. Although it was dark, we could easily see the winged creature as it lifted Meredith off the ground. She was kicking and screaming like crazy.

If Alec and Bobby hadn't acted as fast as they did, Meredith would've been gone. As soon as the bat began to fly off with her, Alec grabbed one of her legs, and Bobby grabbed the other. It seemed impossible, but the bat was able to lift all three of them off the ground!

The weight, however, was too great for the bat. The creature might have succeeded in carrying one person—but not three. He struggled and struggled, pumping his wings harder and harder, but Alec and Bobby held onto Meredith with everything they had. I lunged forward and grabbed Meredith's foot, and Tori grabbed the other one.

It worked. The bat let out an angry squeal and released Meredith. She tumbled to the hard-packed ground, knocking all of us down with her.

"Meredith!" I said. "Are you all right?!?!"

Meredith was dazed, but she seemed unhurt. "I think so," she said.

"But the bat bit you!" Bobby said.

"No, he didn't," Meredith replied. "He only had me by the shirt."

"I can't believe he lifted you off the ground!" I said. "It's like he's bionic, or something!"

"What's 'bionic' mean?" Tori asked.

"It means super-strong," I replied. "It's almost like the bats are part machine."

"They don't look like machines to me," Bobby said. "They look real."

"They *are* real," I said. "What I'm saying is that they have bionic-like strength."

"Let's talk about it later!" Alec said, "after we get to my house. Come on!"

We scrambled to our feet and started off again—but we didn't get far. There was the sound of flapping wings above, and I glanced up just in time to see the hulking silhouettes of more bats in the night sky.

"Here they come again!" I shouted.

"Back to the dugout!" Alec screeched. Gravel and dirt crunched as we spun and began racing back to the dugout. Above us, the sound of flapping wings was getting louder and louder. I could hear squeaks and squeals, and I knew the bats were after us. At any moment, I expected to feel a pair of sharp incisors biting into me and carrying me off.

We reached the dugout and dove in between the benches that were still standing. Quickly, Alec and I tipped up a bench and blocked the thin doorway we'd created.

And just in time, too. The bats swooped down, and one of them actually hit the benches, causing them to wobble. In fact, I thought a few of them were going to fall down, but they didn't.

"That was too close," Meredith said, panting.

"Way too close," Tori echoed.

"All right, change of plans," Alec said. "We'll stay right here. Even if we have to stay the night, we know we'll be safe here in the dugout."

If only Alec had been right.

We weren't safe in the dugout . . . not by a long shot.

19

We were quiet for a long time, just listening to the sounds in the city. While it's not unusual to hear a siren in Bay City (or any city, for that matter), what was strange was how *many* of them we heard. They seemed to be all around us, all over the city, some close, some far away. I didn't like not knowing what was going on, but I was glad the police were doing something about it. I had no clue how they would get rid of the bats, but I was sure they would make the city safe again.

And we'd be safe, too, inside our dugout . . . or, at least, that's what I *thought*.

Meredith finally spoke.

"Thanks, guys," she said quietly. "I really thought that thing was going to carry me away."

"I'm just glad you weren't bitten," Alec said. "Bats can carry rabies, you know."

That was something else that was scary. Rabies is a terrible, deadly disease. If Meredith had been bitten, she would have been in a lot of trouble . . . especially if she couldn't get to the hospital soon.

"Where did they come from?" I asked. "That's what I want to know: How did they suddenly just appear in Bay City? Did they migrate here?"

"What's 'migrate' mean?" Tori asked.

"Don't you know anything?!?!" I snapped, and I was immediately sorry. Tori was a year younger than me, and maybe she didn't know what 'migrate' meant.

"You don't have to be mean to me," she said, sounding hurt.

"I didn't mean to, and I'm sorry." And I was. "'Migrate' means that they travel to different places at different times of the year."

"Like Canada Geese!" she exclaimed.

"Right," I said. "Maybe the bats flew in from somewhere else."

"I don't ever want to see one of those things ever again," Bobby said.

"Well, you just might," I said, "and we have to be prepared. But I think the best thing to do is to stay put. We'll be okay inside this—"

And that's when there was an enormous crash, and all of the benches came tumbling down on us! We could hear squeaks and squeals and flapping wings!

The bats were attacking us in the dugout!

20

We had no warning.

One minute I was talking, and the next minute I was knocked to the ground by tumbling benches. They all seemed to fall at once, like a house of cards, and the five of us were knocked down.

And it hurt! The benches were heavy, and it felt like football players were tackling me. Someone screamed—Tori, I think—but I couldn't be sure. There was too much noise from the benches crashing down.

What made matters worse, of course, was the fact that we couldn't see anything. In the darkness, we were falling all over the place, and soon, the five of us were at the bottom of a pile of fallen benches . . . which was what saved us.

"I can't move!" Bobby exclaimed.

"I can move a little!" Meredith shouted.

"The bats are going to get us!" Tori squealed.

Which wasn't true.

Since all the benches were piled on top of us, the bats couldn't get to us. I don't know how many of them there were—maybe five, maybe ten—but they couldn't get at us. I could hear them screeching angrily and flapping their wings, but they couldn't get at us.

Soon, the bats became frustrated and flew off. I could hear sirens in the distance. My sister was crying, and I felt bad for her.

"Tori?" I asked. "Are you hurt?"

"N . . . n . . . no," she stammered. "I'm scared."

"Don't worry," I said, trying to reassure her. "We're going to get out of this. I won't let anything happen to you."

I heard a clunking sound.

"Man, these things are heavy!" Alec said.

"Can you move?" I asked.

"A little," Alec replied.

"It's a good thing these benches landed on us," I heard Meredith say. "Otherwise, those bats would have been able to get us."

There were more scuffling sounds, and then a loud thud.

"Ouch!" Alec said. "I pushed the bench up, and it landed on my leg! But I think I can get up."

I started squirming and struggling. Although the benches on top of me were too heavy to move, I found I was able to squirm around enough to slip free. Alec and I began working at pulling the benches away and freeing Bobby, Tori, and Meredith.

"Is anyone hurt?" I asked.

"My wrist hurts," Tori sniffed.

"Can you move it?" I replied.

"Yes," she said. "I guess it's not hurt too bad. But it's sore."

"You'll be all right," I said.

"Yeah, but we won't," Bobby replied. "Those bats are going to do anything they can to get at us. If only there was somewhere we could go where we would be safe."

"There is," Alec said. "My house. But we've already tried that."

"Wait a minute!" Bobby said. "Hold everything! I know what we can do!"

And when Bobby explained his idea, I knew that it just might work.

21

"My dad is the volunteer groundskeeper here at the ball field," Bobby said. He was excited, and he spoke quickly.

"But how is he going to help us?" Alec asked.

"He's not," Bobby said. "But one of the things he does is clean the press box and the concession stand over there."

He pointed. About fifty feet from the dugout was a small, two-story building. During games, the bottom part opens up and volunteers sell hot dogs, chips, and soft drinks. The upstairs is a small room where an announcer calls the game.

"I don't see what you mean," Meredith said. "The press box is locked."

"Right," Bobby said. "But Dad says there's a spare key underneath first base. He put one there because he was always forgetting to bring the key. He said he got tired of coming to the ball field, only to have to go back home again to get the key to the press box. If we can get that key, we can get inside the press box! The bats will never be able to get us in there!"

It was a good idea . . . but first base was a long way away. Oh, it wasn't all *that* far . . . but you have to remember that there were bloodthirsty bats patrolling the skies. The plan would be risky.

But right now, it was the only hope we had. We couldn't stay in the dugout, now that we knew the bats could knock down our barricade. In fact, at that very moment, we were still vulnerable, standing in the dugout unprotected. We had to do something . . . and fast.

"But how are we going to get the key?" Tori asked.

"One of us will have to get the key, run to the press box, and unlock it," Alec said.

"Right," Bobby agreed. "I figure it will take less than ten seconds to reach first base and another ten seconds to make it to the press box."

"We should all run together," Alec said. "It would be too dangerous for one person. We all saw what happened to Meredith."

Alec was right. The bats were strong enough to carry a human being. The only thing that saved Meredith was us being able to pull her down. The bat wasn't strong enough to carry all five of us.

"Let's do it," I said. "We'll run together. Bobby—you grab the key from under first base. Then, we'll run to the press box."

My dad has a saying: *Nothing ever goes as planned.* I always wondered why he said that.

I was about to find out why.

22

Nothing ever goes as planned.

I could hear my dad's voice in my head as the five of us prepared to run.

Nothing ever goes as planned, Jamie.

"Everybody ready?" Alec said.

"Wait," Meredith said. "If a bat attacks, we might be able to fend him off. But what if a bunch of bats attack. What then?"

Nobody said anything for a moment. We just listened to the distant wailing sirens. I wondered how many bats there were in the city, and what the police were doing about them. I wondered if anyone had been hurt . . . or worse.

"That's just a chance we'll have to take," I said. "We can't stay here. Even right now, if the bats attacked, we wouldn't be safe. The dugout gives us a little protection, but that's it."

"We could crawl back under the benches," Tori suggested.

And, when I thought about it, that didn't seem like a bad idea. While we had been trapped beneath the benches, the bats weren't able to get to us.

Still, that was too risky. We had no idea just what the bats were capable of or how smart they were. They might figure out a way to pull the benches away from us. After all: they had bionic strength. If they could lift a human into the air, they could lift a wood bench, for sure.

"I like Bobby's idea best," Alec said. "If we can make it to the press box, we'll be safe until help comes. Those bats might be super-strong, but they won't be able to get at us. The building is made of brick."

Right then, I had a really silly thought. I remember reading the story about the three little pigs, and how each one built a house to protect them from the big, bad wolf. One built his home out of straw, and another little pig built his home out of sticks. But the smartest little pig built his home out of brick. The big, bad wolf was able to blow down the first two houses . . . but not the one that was made of brick. Well, I imagined the giant bats huffing and puffing, trying to blow the press box down. It was a goofy thought, I know. But it seemed funny.

What we were about to do, however, wasn't funny. It was serious, and we would have to be careful and be fast.

"Just like last time," Alec said. "We'll go when I count to three. One . . . two . . . *three!*"

The five of us leapt from the dugout and began sprinting across the ball field, down the baseline. We made it to first base in seconds, and Bobby dropped to his knees. In the darkness, I could only see his silhouette, but I could see enough to watch him reach down and flip over the base.

Trouble was, it was dark, and he couldn't see the key.

"It's right here somewhere!" he said frantically. "I know it is!"

"Hurry up!" Meredith said. "Those things might come at any second!"

"Not at any second!" I said, and I pointed to the sky. "Right now! Look! There's four or five of them coming this way!"

"Hurry, Bobby!" Tori urged.

"I'm looking!" Bobby shouted. "It should be here!"

"Find it, fast!" Alec said. "Those things are coming for us!"

"It's no use!" Bobby said. "I can't find the key!"

No key.

No way to get into the press box.

And the bats were coming.

Dad was right: *Nothing ever goes as planned.*

23

I knew we were in a lot of trouble. If we ran back to the dugout, the bats would be able to get at us, now that our barricade of benches had been knocked down. And there wasn't time to crawl underneath the benches, either.

Then, I heard two words of hope:

"GOT IT!"

It was Bobby. He snapped to his feet and stood, holding the key out. I couldn't see it, of course, but I knew he'd finally found it.

"Let's go!" Alec shouted, and we sprang, all five of us, and ran as fast as we could to the press box. I glanced over my shoulder once, only to see the bats circling in the night sky, getting closer and closer.

Just as we reached the press box, a bat flew over my head. He was so close that I could feel air move as he passed by.

"Hurry up, Bobby!" Meredith cried.

"I am, I am!" Bobby shouted.

I heard the key slip into the lock. There were a couple of clicks, then a loud snap. Then, the door was open. Bobby was first inside, then Meredith, followed by Tori, then Alec. I was last, but I was knocked inside! A bat slammed into my back, knocking me forward and into my friends.

But I hadn't been bitten, which was good. More bats were coming at us, and Bobby quickly slammed the door. We heard a bat hit the door, and then another. Then, we heard nothing.

We were in complete darkness for a moment, until Bobby flicked on a light. It was just a single, overhead bulb, but our eyes had adjusted to the dark, and we all squinted. There were a couple tables set up and a small oven that looked really old. Next to it was a white refrigerator. A row of cupboards hung on a wall, and next to the cupboards, a stairway led to the press box. At the bottom of the stairs was a box filled with baseball bats. Otherwise, there really wasn't too much else in the room.

But we were safe. We were safe, and now we could at least see each other.

"We made it!" Meredith exclaimed.

"We were lucky," Alec said. "In fact, we've been *really* lucky."

"Does this place have a phone?" I asked.

Bobby shook his head. "No," he replied. "There's no way we can contact anyone."

"But at least we're all safe," I said. "There's no way the bats can get us now."

We were relieved, that was for sure. Now we knew that we were going to survive. Whatever was going on in the city, however many bats there were, we knew we were going to be all right.

What we didn't know was that we were in for a long night . . . and it all started when we heard a noise from above us.

In the press box.

24

The noise was loud, and we all jumped. Then, we looked at the ceiling, then at the stairs that led up to the press box.

"What was that?" Tori whispered.

"Shhhhh," I replied.

No one moved.

We heard another noise, softer this time. But it definitely came from above us.

"Can the bats get up there?" I whispered to Bobby.

He shook his head. *"No,"* he replied softly. *"There's a big window for the announcer to see out, but it doesn't open."*

The noise came again.

"Well, something's up there," I whispered. *"If it's a giant bat, we're in a lot of trouble."*

"If it's a giant bat, he won't be able to fly," Alec said quietly. *"He won't have enough room."*

"How would he have gotten in?" Meredith asked. *"This place was locked."*

"Maybe it's another person," I said. *"Bobby . . . is there anyone else who has a key to this place?"*

Bobby shook his head. *"Just my dad,"* he replied.

Another scraping sound came from above, and something small crashed to the floor. Again, we flinched.

"Well, something is up there," Alec whispered, *"and we'd better find out what it is."*

"I'm not going up there," Tori said.

"Me neither," Meredith echoed.

"*I'm not going to go, either,*" Bobby said.

"*I'll go,*" Alec said, and I was glad. I didn't want to go upstairs, either, and I was relieved when Alec volunteered.

Turns out, Alec didn't have to go upstairs, after all . . . because at that moment, there was a sudden scratching sound, and the creature came down the steps!

25

I'll tell you this much:

We never expected to see what we were seeing. We had thought that perhaps a bionic bat had somehow gotten inside.

Wrong.

It was only a *chipmunk!*

He bounced down the steps and scurried into a little hole in the corner. I think we scared him worse than he scared us!

I burst out laughing. Soon, all of us were roaring. Sometimes, when you think the worst and nothing bad happens, you wonder why you ever thought it in the first place.

"Come on," Bobby said. "Let's check out upstairs."

Bobby walked to the staircase, turned on another light, and started up the steps. The rest of us followed.

The press box didn't have much in it. There was a table with two microphones and some electrical equipment. There was a calendar on the wall, along with a plaque, congratulating someone on being 'Announcer of the Year'. On the floor, we found what the chipmunk had knocked over: a small, cup-like pencil-holder. There were about a half-dozen pens and pencils scattered on the floor. On the table, there was a baseball score sheet that read:

Pirates 24
Lizards 1

"Man," Alec said, looking at the score sheet. "The Lizards sure got their clocks cleaned."

There really wasn't anything special about the press box, except for the fact that the window gave us a clear view of not only the ball field, but houses nearby. Almost everyone had their lights on, which seemed odd.

But, then again, everybody in the entire city was probably freaked out by the giant bats. I doubted there was a single person in Bay City sleeping through this nightmare.

We could still hear sirens in the distance, and on the next block over, we caught a glimpse of flashing red and blue lights. They appeared like a firefly and vanished just as quickly.

"You're sure there's not a phone or a radio in this place?" Alec asked Bobby.

Bobby shook his head. "No, there's not. Dad always has to use his cell phone when he calls from here."

"We need to find a way to let someone know we're here," Meredith said. "If the police knew we were here, I bet they would come and get us. They would drive us home."

"Yeah, but without a phone or a radio, that'll be impossible," Bobby said.

I looked at the table, at the score sheet, and the equipment.

"Hey!" I blurted out. "I know what we can do! I know how we can let people know we're here!"

26

On the desk were two microphones . . . and a public address system.

"Guys!" I said. "We can use the public address system to let people know we're here! The announcers use it during ball games to announce scores and stuff! The speakers are mounted on telephone poles outside! We can turn up the volume really loud and let everyone know that we need help!"

"That's a great idea!" Bobby said. "The houses on the other side of the field will be able to hear us for sure!"

"They can call the police and let them know we need help!" said Meredith.

"Do you know how to work the sound system?" I asked Bobby.

Bobby shrugged. "Not really. But I've seen the announcers use it before. It shouldn't be too hard."

He stepped forward to the table, reached out, and flicked a switch on one of the pieces of electronics. Tiny lights blinked on. Some of them flashed repeatedly.

"I think," Bobby said as he leaned down to the microphone, "all we have to do is talk into this. Hello? Hello? Is this on?"

We didn't hear anything except Bobby's plain voice.

"Where's the volume control?" I asked.

Bobby pointed. "It's right there," he said, and he turned the knob. "Hello? Hello? Testing, one, two, three . . . ."

Still, we didn't hear anything. Bobby's voice sounded as normal as ever.

Tori reached out and flipped a tiny switch on the microphone. "What's this thing do?" she asked.

Bobby spoke into the microphone again, but his voice was loud!

"Hello . . . hey! It works!" His booming voice came from the speakers outside the press box, and we could hear his words echoing across the neighborhood.

"It's working!" Alec said. "Are there any outside lights? That would help draw attention."

Bobby shook his head. "No," he said. "My dad says that all the teams are trying to raise money to buy lights, so they can have games after dark. But they don't have enough money, yet."

"Say something," I said. "Let people know we're here!"

Bobby spoke into the microphone, and his boomy voice carried over the dark ball field.

"CAN ANYONE HEAR ME?!?! WE'RE TRAPPED IN THE PRESS BOX AT THE BASEBALL FIELD! IS THERE ANYONE WHO CAN HEAR ME?!?! PLEASE,

HELP US! THERE ARE FIVE OF US IN THE PRESS BOX AT THE BASEBALL FIELD!"

He stopped speaking, and we watched and listened. I was hoping to see a shadow come to one of the lit windows in one of the homes across from the ball field, but none came.

"Try again," Alec said. "Someone's got to hear you."

"CAN ANYONE HEAR ME?!?! PLEASE, HELP US! THERE ARE FIVE OF US TRAPPED IN THE PRESS BOX! WE CAN'T LEAVE, BECAUSE OF THE BATS! IF ANYONE CAN HEAR ME, PLEASE HELP!"

As soon as he stopped speaking, a light blinked on in one of the houses.

A silhouette appeared at the window.

"Someone heard you!" Tori shouted.

"IF YOU CAN HEAR ME, PLEASE HELP US!" Bobby pleaded into the microphone. *"WE'RE TRAPPED OVER HERE IN THE PRESS BOX!"*

The figure vanished, and we waited.

"I'll bet he's calling the police right now!" Alec said. "I'll bet they come and save us with a bunch of police cars!"

Suddenly, we heard a muffled *bang*. It was very faint, but there was no doubt about what it was.

A screen door banging shut.

Then, a flashlight clicked on in front of the house where we'd seen the shadow.

Someone had come outside, and now he was walking toward us!

"Oh, no!" Meredith shrieked. "Doesn't he know about the bats?!?!"

"He will in a minute!" I shouted, tapping the window as I pointed up into the night sky. "Here they come!"

27

Bobby didn't waste another moment. He leaned closer to the microphone.

"GO BACK!" he shouted. *"THERE ARE GIANT BATS ALL OVER THE PLACE! GO BACK INSIDE!"*

We couldn't see the person, but the flashlight beam suddenly stopped moving.

"GO BACK!" Bobby ordered. *"THERE ARE GIANT BATS COMING FOR YOU!"*

Now, I didn't know who was coming to help us, but it was obvious he wasn't aware of the danger, because we saw the flashlight beam moving again . . . toward us!

High above, in the night sky, I could see the dark silhouettes of several bats as they circled their unsuspecting prey.

Then, we heard a voice. It was faint and hard to hear being that we were in the press box, but we could hear a man speaking.

"You kids are going to get into big trouble, playing a joke like this!" he said angrily. "When I find out who you are, I'm going to call your parents!"

"IT'S NO JOKE!" Bobby pleaded into the microphone. *"YOU HAVE TO BELIEVE ME! THERE ARE GIANT BATS ATTACKING BAY CITY! SOME OF THEM ARE RIGHT ABOVE YOU, RIGHT NOW!"*

Still, the man kept coming. It was, of course, very dark . . . but he looked like he was nearing the ball field.

Above, a horrific winged creature dropped out of the sky.

Then another.

One more.

"PLEASE, MISTER!" Bobby shouted. *"THIS IS NOT A JOKE! RUN FOR YOUR LIFE!"*

The man spoke again. "When I get hold of you, I'm going to—"

Suddenly, he screamed.

His flashlight fell to the ground and went out.

It was all over for the angry man with the flashlight.

28

I felt horrible.

The man was being attacked by giant bats, and it was *our* fault!

"We shouldn't have called for help!" Meredith said. "The bats attacked him, and it was all because of *us!*"

"Hey, we didn't know anyone would come outside!" Bobby said. "He must not have known about the bats!"

"We've got to do something," I said.

"What can we do?" Alec said. "If we go outside, we're going to be goners . . . just like that dude with the flashlight."

One by one, we saw the bats heading back up into the sky, but they were too far away to see if one of them was carrying the man.

"That was horrible!" Tori said, and she started to cry a little bit. "That man didn't deserve that."

We all felt awful, and we began to realize how desperate our situation had become. Who knew how many bats had invaded the city? Where had they come from? How would they be stopped?

And we were prisoners in a press box. How long would it take for someone to rescue us?

"Well," Bobby said, "the good thing is, we have plenty of water and food. That is, of course, if you don't mind eating cold hotdogs from the fridge downstairs."

"And potato chips," Meredith added.

"I'm not very hungry," I said.

"Me neither," Alec chimed in. "I think I've lost my appetite for a month."

"Well, we won't be here that long," Bobby said.

"How do you know?" Meredith asked. She sounded angry. "We don't know anything about what's going on. There might be a lot of people trapped just like us, waiting for help to arrive. We might be stuck here for *days*. If we try to get out of here, those ginormous birds are going to get us."

It was a scary thought.

"Bats aren't birds," Alec said flatly.

"I don't care what they are!" Meredith said. "I want them to go away!"

"We're just going to have to wait it out," I said. "Let's not argue about it."

"I'm not arguing," Meredith said. "I just want to be home. I want to go to sleep tonight in my own bed and wake up in my own room!" She was really angry . . . and scared.

But we *all* were. All we could do was hope for the best.

Until we saw a bat, flying low over the baseball field. In the moonlight, I could see his glistening eyes. I could see his powerful wings flapping.

And with every passing millisecond, our fear went up a notch.

Further.

The bat seemed to be looking at us.

Worse—he was coming right at us.

"He's . . . he's not turning!" Bobby exclaimed.

"He's speeding up!" I shouted.

"Everybody look out!" Alec wailed. *"He's going to try to smash through the press box window!"*

29

We scattered every which way, bumping into each other as we tried to get away from the window. The bat was only moments from slamming into the window, and it was clear he wasn't turning away.

We all managed to reach the stairs . . . just as the bat struck the press box. There was a loud shattering sound, and a gabillion glass shards flew everywhere. I heard Bobby wail a sharp *"ouch!"*

I turned. The bat had succeeded in breaking the window, but didn't make it into the press box.

But I knew he would, eventually. He'd broken the glass and was now preparing to fly in after us,

I was sure. He—and probably more bats— were going to get us, if we didn't act fast.

At the bottom of the stairs, Alec pulled out a baseball bat from the box. He tossed it into the air while shouting *"Jamie! Catch!"* If I hadn't acted quickly, the bat would have hit me in the face.

But I could understand what he was doing, as he handed bats to everyone else.

"Use them to defend yourselves if they get inside!" Alec said.

A funny thought came to my mind.

I've heard of fighting fire with fire . . . but we're fighting bats . . . with bats. If I hadn't been so scared at the time, I probably would've laughed my head off.

We're fighting bats . . . with bats.

But I was glad that Alec had been smart enough to think about the baseball bats in the box, because I'd no sooner grasped the handle than a bat swooped by the front of the press box. He didn't try to get in, but I knew it was only a matter of time. There was no glass in the window—it was all over the floor, in millions of sharp pieces.

Downstairs, I heard Alec call out: "Jamie! Fend off the bats until we can get a table up there!"

"What are you talking about?!?!" I shouted back.

"Bobby and I will bring a table up!" Alec replied. "It will be big enough to cover most of the window!"

"I can't fight the bats by myself!" I shouted.

Just then, Meredith appeared. She was carrying a blue-colored aluminum baseball bat.

And she looked *mad.*

"You won't have to fight them by yourself," she said angrily. "Let's get 'em!"

"You shouldn't be up here," I said to her.

"What's *that* supposed to mean?!?!" she spat.

"Nothing," I said. "But . . . I mean, you're . . . you're a—"

"—a girl?!?!" she finished. "You think I can't take care of myself?!?!"

"No, it's not that. I, uh, I guess—"

"Listen, Jamie. I can use this bat just as good as *you* can. And I intend to!"

"Go get 'em, slugger," I mumbled.

We stood a few feet apart, in front of what once had been a large, rectangular glass window. The night was growing cooler, and the air chilled my skin. With the window now open, we could hear the sirens once again. And some shouting in the distance, as well.

And we also heard something else:

Flapping wings.

"Get ready, Meredith," I said, trying to sound calm. "Here they come!"

30

The bats came at us like winged rockets . . . but we were ready for them.

"There's one!" Meredith shrieked as a bat emerged from the darkness, heading straight for us. I swung my bat over my shoulder, ready for battle—but Meredith was faster. In fact, she didn't even swing her bat . . . she just used it as a poker, of sorts. The flying bat hit the aluminum baseball bat, squealed, and flew off.

"Good job!" I said, just as another bat attacked. I did the same thing Meredith had done: instead of swinging the bat, I poked it at the attacking beast.

I caught him right below his neck, and the blow not only stopped his attack, but it kept him out of the press box.

But I knew we wouldn't be able to do this for long. If two or more bats attacked at the same time, we'd never be able to fend them off.

"Hurry it up with that table, you guys!" I shouted over my shoulder. "This isn't a picnic, you know!"

"This thing's heavy!" I heard Bobby call out from below. "We're moving as fast as we can!"

"It's not fast enough!" I hollered back as I spotted another bat coming in for an attack. Meredith and I teamed up on this one. The bat sped toward us, and when he tried to fly into the press box, we used the baseball bats like swords to divert him away. It worked—but there were still more bats coming.

Bobby and Alec appeared in the stairway. They'd folded the legs in on the long table and were trying to get it up to the press box. Tori was helping to push, but the table was big. They were having a tough time wrangling it up the stairs, but they were managing.

"Hurry!" I shouted as two more bats flew toward us. They were really moving fast, too, and I hoped we'd be able to fend them off.

Bobby reached the top of the stairs, grunting and groaning as he pulled the table. Broken glass crunched beneath his feet. The two bats swooped in for the attack, but Meredith and I were ready. We wielded the baseball bats before us, gripping them like our very lives depended on them.

In fact, our lives *did* depend on them!

The flying creatures came at us with such fury that I thought both of them would succeed in coming into the press box. But, using the baseball bats as weapons, we were somehow able to keep the hideous flying beasts away. They squealed up into the night sky—but more were still coming.

By now, Bobby, Tori, and Alec had succeeded in getting the table into the press box. With its legs folded in, it was long and flat. It wouldn't cover the entire broken window, but most of it. There would be a small area at the top of the window that the table wouldn't cover, but I didn't think it would be big enough for the bats to get through.

"Help us get this in front of the window!" Alec said. I made a quick glance into the night sky to make sure no bats were coming. I saw one, but, with any luck, we'd be able to get the table up in time.

Meredith and I dropped the bats, and they clunked to the floor. We grabbed the table top by the edges and lifted. It wasn't very heavy with the five of us lifting it, but it was bulky.

"He's coming! He's coming!" Tori squealed.

Just as soon as we got the table top in position, the bat slammed into it, knocking us all a little backward. However, the force wasn't enough to knock us to the ground.

"Bobby!" Alec shouted. "Grab one of those long pieces of wood on the far wall! We'll use it to prop against the table to keep it in place!"

Bobby scrambled to the other side of the room. Broken glass crunched and popped beneath his feet. He picked up one of the long boards and took it to Alec. Alec took the board and propped one end on the floor where it met the wall and the other end against the table.

"Another one!" Alec ordered. Again, Bobby grabbed a board and handed it to Alec, who repeated the process of leaning the board against the table top. This time, however, it was on the other side.

"There," he said, taking a step back. "That will hold it."

Just as he spoke, a bat slammed into the table. We didn't see it coming, of course—but the table held.

We were safe—at least for now.

31

I have to admit . . . we all got more and more worried as time passed. Sure, we were safe inside the press box. The lights worked, so we weren't in the dark . . . but we had no idea what was going on around us. There was no radio or television in the press box, so we couldn't get any news reports. It seemed the only thing we could do was wait.

"We could try the microphone again," I said. We'd all been standing around, not saying much of anything. Waiting. Hoping.

"I don't know," Alec said. "After what happened to that guy."

That made us all stop and think. That poor guy hadn't had a chance. It was as if he didn't have any idea that giant bats had invaded the city.

"Anybody know what time it is?" I asked.

No one did. None of us had a watch.

"It's probably around eleven o'clock," Alec said.

"Man, my mom and dad are probably freaking out right now," Bobby said.

I thought about that. I tried to imagine what my parents were doing at that very moment. They were worried sick, I was sure.

"Why hasn't anyone come to look for us?" Meredith asked.

"My guess is that the police have ordered everyone to stay at home," Alec replied. "It would be too dangerous for people to be outside their homes."

We could still hear sirens in the distance. We also heard a sudden flapping of wings and a snarl, and we knew that a bat had just flown past the press box. They knew we were in here, that was for sure.

All we had to do was wait it out. Sooner or later, someone would come looking for us. Even if we had to wait all night. The worst was over, I was sure. This whole nightmare would be over in the morning.

Boy, was I wrong about *that.*

Tori began to speak. "I'm thirsty," she said. "I'm going downstairs to get some water. Anybody else want—"

There was a sudden, thundering crash as something slammed into the table that covered the broken window.

Oh, we knew what that something was, all right. But we knew he couldn't get in: after all, we'd already planned for that.

But when I saw the bat's head begin squirming in the open space between the table and the top of the window, I again heard the voice of my father speaking.

Nothing ever goes as planned . . . .

151

32

Alec and I were the first to react, snapping up baseball bats. The creature was making an awful racket: snarling and squealing, claws scraping at the table.

The worst of it was the fact that he was actually succeeding in squeezing through the open space between the table and the window!

"Push him back!" Alec shouted, and we began using the baseball bats to poke and push the bat back outside. By now, the beast had already been able to wriggle halfway through. His mouth was open, snapping from side to side. I couldn't imagine what it would feel like if those awful teeth sunk into my flesh.

Bobby picked up a baseball bat, and he, too, began poking and prying at the creature.

"We need more help!" I shrieked.

Meredith picked up a baseball bat, and Tori did, too. With the five of us all working to keep the bat out, we succeeded . . . but another bat quickly took his place.

"That's not fair!" Bobby shouted. "They're ganging up on us!"

"Of course it's fair!" Alec shouted as he pried and pushed at the creature with the baseball bat. "They can do whatever they want! They're bionic bats!"

The second bat that tried to get in was even bigger than the first one. He couldn't squeeze in very far, and we were able to fend him off. But again, yet another bat appeared in the space, flapping and going crazy, trying to wriggle inside and get to us.

I began to realize how hopeless our situation was. Here we were, five kids, trying to defend ourselves from these huge creatures . . . with baseball bats. The beasts were as big as we were, but they were probably a lot stronger. And we had no idea how many there were. There might be a hundred, there might be a thousand. Maybe ten thousand. The only thing we had going for us was that we were smarter, and we'd been really lucky—so far.

Now, however, it appeared that our luck was tapped out.

"Keep pushing!" Meredith shouted as the bat succeeded in getting one entire wing into the press box. The single wing flapped like crazy.

I was next to Alec, and we were using the fat ends of our baseball bats to push the creature's shoulders back, trying to keep him from getting even further inside.

It wasn't working.

With an awful snarl and a surge of energy, the bat made an enormous effort and succeeded in getting his other wing inside the press box.

"Everybody downstairs!" I shrieked. *"He's coming inside, whether we like it or not!"*

A bad night was about to get a lot worse.

33

Realizing there was nothing more we could do, we scrambled down the stairs like mad ants. I had no idea how we were going to defend ourselves, but the first thing we needed to do was get away from the creature. Maybe the five of us could fend him off in the concession stand; maybe not. Maybe we would be forced to leave the small building entirely.

Which, of course, would put us in more danger. If we had to leave the safety of the press box, we'd be out in the open . . . where more bats would surely come after us.

We made it downstairs and ran to the far wall. All of us still had our baseball bats in our hands, ready to use them. Not that it would do much good, but it made me feel a *little* bit better that I had *something* to use to defend myself.

Upstairs, we could hear the bat struggling and thrashing about.

"He's going to get us!" Tori shrieked.

"Maybe not," Alec said. "He's too big to fly in here. His wings are too wide. He might be able to get in, but he won't be able to fly . . . and bats can't walk or crawl well at all."

I sure hoped Alec was right!

Outside, I heard a siren wail. It drew closer and closer, until I was sure that it must've passed right by the baseball field!

"Maybe they're coming to save us!" Meredith cried.

"Let's hope so," I said, but our hopes faded when the siren continued wailing, sounding farther and farther away with each moment. It was an emergency vehicle, all right . . . but it had been on its way to someplace else. I figured we weren't the only people who had an emergency. There were probably lots of people in trouble, just like us.

Upstairs, we could hear the bat banging and clanging around. Whether he could fly or not, he was still dangerous. I didn't want to get into a wrestling match with anything that had fangs longer than my hands!

"Everybody get ready!" Alec said.

The five of us stood at the far wall opposite the steps. Each one of us had a baseball bat. We were all shaking like leaves. Tori was crying a little, but she was acting brave.

There was silence from the press box upstairs. The only things we could hear were the constant whine of distant sirens and the heavy gasps of our own deep breaths.

Then, we heard a shuffling sound from above, and a dull thud.

"Here he comes," Alec breathed. *"Stay ready."*

We thought we were ready for anything. As we stood trembling, ready to wield our baseball bats as weapons, we were as ready as ready could be.

However, Alec had been wrong: the bat in the press box *could* fly.

And we weren't ready for it when it flew down the stairwell and came right at us . . . .

34

What came at us wasn't huge.

It wasn't a bloodthirsty, gigantic creature.

It was an ordinary brown bat, no bigger than a sparrow!

The sight of the bat surprised all of us, and we all jumped. But the bat didn't attack us; rather, he only circled above our heads, flapping his wings, darting around the room. Then, he flew back up the stairwell and into the press box.

We stood stunned, holding our baseball bats before us.

"Was . . . was that . . . was that the same bat?" I stammered.

"Couldn't have been," Alec said. "That was just an ordinary bat."

"Shhhh," Meredith whispered. "Maybe the big one is still upstairs."

We listened, but heard nothing.

"Do you think the bat shrank?" Bobby asked Alec.

Alec shook his head. "It's not possible," Alec said. "There's no way."

"Yeah, well, we would've thought ginormous bats were impossible, too," Meredith said. "But we saw them with our own eyes. They've been after us all night."

"Could it be that the giant bats are nothing more than overgrown brown bats?" I asked Alec.

"No," he said, "it's just not possible. Bats just don't get that big."

"Tell that to the guy across the street," I said.

Just then, we heard the sound of loud flapping wings as they swept over the press box.

"See?" Alec said. "Whatever they are, they're still out there, just as big as ever. You guys wait here. I'll go upstairs and see what's up."

"Be careful," I said.

Alec strode cautiously to the stairs and slowly walked up the steps, holding the baseball bat in front of him. Soon, all we could see were his shoes.

"Nothing up here at all," he called out. "Even the little bat is gone. He must've flown out the space between the table and the window."

Sure, it sounded crazy—but everything about the night had been crazy.

"Well," Tori began, "maybe if *that* bat shrank, they all will," she said.

"Let's hope so," I told her.

Alec came back down. "That was a close one," he said. "I think the best thing we can do now is just wait. Sooner or later, someone will find us."

"I'm tired," Tori said. She sat on the floor and leaned back against the wall. Meredith sat down next to her. Soon, we were all seated on the floor.

Soon, we were all tired.

Soon, we'd all fallen asleep—and that's something we shouldn't have done.

35

I was awakened by a loud rumble, and I was immediately confused . . . but only for a moment. Then, I realized what had happened and where I was.

The noise woke everyone else, too. Everyone had fallen asleep on the floor. I had been leaning against the wall and my head had slumped forward so that my chin was resting on my chest. My neck was tight and sore.

"What was that?" Tori asked sleepily.

"Sounded like thunder," Alec replied. And, indeed, it was. I could hear a steady rain pattering on the roof, and there was another rumble of thunder off in the distance.

"I wonder what time it is," Bobby said with a yawn.

"Couldn't tell you," I said. "We can't see outside, so we don't even know if it's morning yet."

"How come no one has come to help us?" Meredith asked. "I mean . . . our parents must have told the police we were missing. But no one has come looking for us."

"Like I said earlier," Alec said, "I think the police have ordered everyone to stay inside. They won't want anyone going out until it's safe."

He stood, stretched, walked over to the stairs, and took a few steps up. He craned his neck and looked into the press box.

"Still dark out," he said, and then he came back down and sat on the floor. "It could be midnight, it could be three in the morning."

"But we're all still alive," Meredith said.

"Yeah, it could be a lot worse," I replied. "We could have—"

"Shhh!" Alec hissed. "Hear that?"

We listened. I could hear a police siren, which wasn't unusual: we'd been hearing them all night.

What *was* unusual is that it was coming closer and closer!

We leapt to our feet, sprinted to the stairs, and sprang up the steps, bumping into one another. The five of us raced to the window where the table was still propped against it, and we peered out the space between the top of the table and the window.

On the other side of the baseball field was a police car! Its lights were flashing, and the trees and houses reflected the intermittent blue and red splashes.

"Get on the microphone!" Alec said.

Bobby went to the desk and leaned down. "HELP US!" he shouted. "PLEASE HELP US! WE'RE IN THE PRESS BOX!"

Suddenly, a spotlight clicked on, and it was aimed right at us. I raised my arm to shield my eyes from the bright light.

And then:

A voice! A big, booming voice came from a loudspeaker in the patrol car!

"ARE ALL OF YOU ALL RIGHT?!?!"

"YES!" Bobby answered into the microphone. "BUT WE'VE BEEN TRAPPED HERE ALL NIGHT BECAUSE OF THE BATS!"

"HOW MANY OF YOU ARE THERE?" the voice from the patrol car responded.

"FIVE OF US!" Bobby said, and his voice echoed through the neighborhood.

"STAY WHERE YOU ARE, AND WE'LL BRING A POLICE VAN TO THE DOOR," the policeman ordered. Then, the spotlight clicked off, and the car pulled away.

We cheered. We were going to be rescued. Our nightmare was over—almost.

The bats weren't going to let us get away that easily . . . not without a fight.

36

Our night of madness was nearly over, and, very soon, we would all be going home.

"I don't think I've ever been happier in my whole life!" Tori cheered. "I thought we were going to be stuck here all night!"

"Me, too," Bobby said. "I'm glad that policeman came along when he did."

"Let's go wait by the door," Alec said. "The police will probably be here soon."

We scurried down the stairs, feeling excited and anxious.

Nothing ever goes as planned, I thought. We sure found that out tonight, in a big way.

But at least we were safe, and we were going home. Nothing had gone as planned tonight, that's for sure. What started out as a game of hide-and-seek turned into another game altogether: a dangerous game where we had to fight to stay alive.

And thankfully, it was a game we'd won . . . at least, that's what I thought.

Until we heard a loud crash from upstairs and an angry squeal. Then, another loud crash, which was the unmistakable sound of the table crashing to the floor.

"They're attacking again!" Meredith shrieked.

"Quick!" Alec shouted. "Everybody grab a baseball bat!"

We scurried around the inside of the concession stand and picked up bats. Then, we all huddled next to one another, near the door, ready to get out as soon as the police van arrived.

Upstairs, we could hear more thrashing and clanging. More snarling and squealing.

"He's too big," Alec said reassuringly. "He can't fly in such a small space."

"But that other bat shrank," I reminded him. "Maybe this one will, too."

Well, the bat in the press box didn't shrink, and it didn't fly . . . but it was coming down the steps! We were horrified when the giant bat (looking more like a monster than anything else) slowly slunk down the stairs. His wings were folded in, and he was walking on his hind legs. His movements were awkward and uncertain, but that wasn't stopping him. And when he opened his mouth and showed his fangs, I think all five of us nearly fainted. He howled and hissed when he made it to the bottom of the steps, and we knew he was only seconds away from an all-out attack.

"Open the door!" I said. "We're going to have to make a run for it!"

"But the police aren't here, yet!" Bobby cried.

Alec opened the door a tiny bit. "Yes, they are!" he exclaimed. "They're coming! I can see the van a few blocks away!"

The bat sprang forward, and we had no choice but to flee. Even if it meant risking an attack by other bats outside.

Alec flung the door all the way open, and we scrambled out. The ground was still wet from the rain, and I could see puddles in the dirt parking lot.

"Run!" Alec shouted. "We can make it to the van!"

We sprang, running across the parking lot, not even trying to dodge the numerous puddles that reflected the glowing streetlights above. None of us had dropped our baseball bats, either—just in case we had to use them again.

Behind us, the bat that had been in the press box had also emerged from the open door. Now he was flying—and he was coming after us!

Up ahead, the van was getting closer and closer. The side door slid open, and there were two uniformed police officers ready to help us.

Bobby reached the van first, and he dove inside. Meredith was next, then Tori.

The bat came at me. I knew he was close, and I knew that I might not make it to the van if I didn't do something.

I spun and raised the baseball bat . . . and that's what probably saved my life. The creature was swooping down, mouth open, attacking. However, instead of biting me, he clamped down on the aluminum baseball bat!

I let it go, spun, and followed Alec into the waiting van, where the police officers grabbed us and slid the door closed.

Finally, after what seemed to be a never-ending nightmare, we were safe.

We were going home.

37

The police didn't tell us too much about what was going on, because they said they didn't know themselves. All they said was that giant bats had overtaken the city, and everyone had been ordered to stay inside. They asked where we lived and took us all to our houses. The driver parked the van as close to the front door as possible, and the two policemen escorted us to the house, just in case we came under attack by more bats. Thankfully, we didn't.

And were our parents happy to see us! Mom cried, and so did Tori. I might have cried—just a little bit. I sure was glad to be safe in our own home.

Merlin, Tori's cat, was safe, too. Mom said she'd let Merlin inside shortly after we left the night before, so he'd been indoors and out of harm's way.

The next day, the story about Bay City and the bionic bats was big news all across the country. It was also the day we found out what had happened, and why.

Apparently, a sugar beet farmer not far from Bay City had been trying an experimental fertilizer to help his crop grow bigger and faster. Bay City is famous for sugar beets, and there are many sugar beet farms in the region.

Well, the farmer's experimental fertilizer worked. But the leaves of the plants gave off some particular smell that only bats could sense. It made them ravenously hungry, and, although bats normally only eat bugs, thousands of them swarmed down on the farm and ate the leaves of the growing sugar beet plants. The fertilizer in the ground had caused a chain-reaction in the plants, which caused the bats to grow to enormous size within hours. I didn't understand all the particulars, but I saw lots of scientists on television explaining how it had happened. The good news, however, was that the effects on the bats wore off within twenty-four hours, and the bats had now returned to normal size. On television, we watched footage of police and other workers at the farmer's field, destroying the remaining crop so that the bats could no longer eat the leaves. They even interviewed the farmer, and he said he was really sorry and embarrassed. He said it was an accident, and he wouldn't be using his experimental fertilizer ever again.

And no one was hurt seriously. We found out that the man we thought had been carried away by bats hadn't been carried away, after all. He'd been sleeping when we awakened him with the public address system and had no idea that Bay City was under attack by giant bats. That's why he thought we were just a bunch of kids causing trouble.

Anyway, the bats *had* attacked him. He'd dropped his flashlight and it broke, but it was one of those big, long, heavy flashlights. He was able to use it against the bats and make it back to his home safely.

That morning, the curfew on the city was lifted, and people were allowed to leave their homes. There were no more giant bats, and things could now begin to get back to normal.

Meredith called around noon.

"I'm going down to the river to let Clyde go," she said. "You want to come?"

"Sure," I said. "I'll meet you there."

After lunch, I went into the garage and hopped on my bike. The day was sunny and very, very warm. As I rode down the block, all I could think about were the giant bats and what had happened to the five of us. We'd been really lucky, and I would never forget how scared we'd all been.

But there was nothing to worry about anymore. The giant bats were gone. The effects of the sugar beet leaves had worn off, and now they'd all returned to their original, puny size.

Except for one.

The sun was at my back, and my shadow bobbed in front of my bike.

But another shadow came into view.

A huge shadow—*with wings!*

38

I swerved so quickly that I nearly fell off my bike. Then, I started peddling as fast as I could, until the shadow was gone.

Finally, I turned my head and looked up over my shoulder.

A seagull.

That's all I was. It was drifting low, riding an air current. It was big, and its shadow on the ground had made it appear even bigger.

I should've known, I thought. *Sheesh.*

A few minutes later, I met Meredith at the river. She had placed Clyde on the riverbank, not far from the water. The turtle moved slowly and didn't seem in too much of a hurry.

"I still can't believe that happened last night," Meredith said. "It seems like it was all a dream."

"I know," I agreed. "It doesn't seem real. Maybe someone should write a book about it."

"Maybe *you* should," Meredith said, pointing at me. "After all, you were *there*. You *know* what happened to all of us."

"I might," I said. "There are lots of other weird stories about strange things that have happened in Michigan. This could sure count as one of them."

We watched Clyde as he ambled down the embankment and slipped into the water. He vanished in seconds.

"I'm going to miss him," Meredith said. "But he belongs in the wild. I'm sure he's happier in the river."

We said good-bye, and I began peddling home. The sun was really hot on my skin, and I thought it would be a great day to run through some sprinklers. On hot days like this, most of our neighbors turn their sprinklers on. We don't have any lakes or pools nearby, so the sprinklers are a great way to stay cool on really hot days.

Rounding the corner onto our block, I saw a girl sitting on the curb. Her bicycle was a few feet from her, laying sideways on the grass. As I drew closer, I could see her hands were dark and grease-stained.

I slowed to a stop. "What's wrong?" I asked.

She turned. "My chain came off," she said, "and I can't get it back on."

I hopped off my bike. The girl didn't look familiar, and I figured she was new or just visiting someone.

"I can probably fix it for you," I said.

"That would be great," the girl said. "I've been trying for ten minutes."

"I'm Jamie," I said, and I leaned over and stood her bike up.

The girl stood. "I'm Mikayla," she replied. "We just moved here from Calumet."

Calumet? I wondered. I'd never heard of the place. "Where's that?" I asked.

"It's way up in the Upper Peninsula, a long ways from here," she replied. "Mom took a job here. We moved into our new apartment just last week."

I flipped her bicycle over. The chain was stuck between the sprocket and the frame, but I was able to free it.

"There you go," I said as I turned the pedal with my hand. The chain caught on the sprocket, and the back wheel began to turn.

"Thank you so much," she said, getting to her feet. "I thought I was going to have to push it home."

We talked for a couple more minutes, and I pointed to my house down the street. "That's where I live," I said.

"I live about six blocks from here," Mikayla said. "I got bored, so I thought I'd go for a bike ride and check out the neighborhood."

"So, you were here last night when the giant bats attacked the city?" I asked.

Mikayla nodded. "Yes, we were," she said. "It was the scariest thing that my brother and I have ever gone through . . . almost."

"What do you mean 'almost'?" I replied.

"Before we moved, we had something much scarier happen to us in Calumet," she said.

"What could be scarier than giant bats with huge fangs?" I asked her.

"Creatures in the ground," Mikayla replied, very seriously. "You see, Calumet used to be known for its copper mines. Most of the mines are all closed down, but they're still there."

"So, what's so scary about that?" I asked again.

"Tell you what," Mikayla said, hopping on her bike. "Let's go for a bike ride. I'll tell you all about it."

That sounded good. I hopped onto my bike, and we started out.

"Everything began when my brother and I decided to go hiking in the woods with friends," she began. As we pedaled around the block and along city streets, Mikayla told me a truly terrifying story . . . about the Calumet Copper Creatures . . . .

NEXT IN THE
MICHIGAN CHILLERS SERIES:

#15: CALUMET
COPPER
CREATURES

CONTINUE ON TO READ A FEW
CHILLING CHAPTERS!

1

"Mom, have you seen my hiking shoes?" my brother called out. He'd been looking for them for ten minutes, and he still hadn't found them.

"Have you checked the garage, Calvin?" Mom asked. She was in the living room, putting on her sweater, getting ready to go shopping in town.

"I'll look again," Calvin said, as he strode through the kitchen and through the side door that led to the garage.

"Mikayla," Mom said to me, "you keep an eye on him while I'm gone. Don't let him get into trouble like last week."

I rolled my eyes. "Yes, Mom," I said. Last week while Mom had been on her weekly shopping trip, Calvin was hitting rocks with an old tennis racket. One of the rocks broke a window in a house across the street. Oh, it was an accident. Calvin didn't mean to do it. But the window was still broken. Calvin didn't have enough money to pay for it, so Mom had to. Calvin was paying Mom back over the summer by doing odd jobs around the house.

And I got into a little trouble, too. I'm eleven, and Calvin is eight. I was supposed to be watching him, but I had been on the phone, talking to a friend. Oh, I knew what Calvin was doing. I could see him in the yard, swinging the racket at stones he was tossing into the air . . . but I never thought he might actually break a window.

Mom left to go shopping in town. We live in Calumet, which is a city in Michigan's Upper Peninsula. It's a great place to live, but you'd better like snow. We get a *ton* of it in the winter! Sometimes, we get so much snow that the city streets look like tunnels after they've been plowed.

And summers are great. Calumet is small, compared to some of Michigan's larger cities, and it's surrounded by lots of woods. Plus, Lake Superior is only a few miles away. There are lots more smaller lakes around, too. Sometimes, my brother and I go fishing or swimming in them.

But Calumet used to be known for something else: copper. You see, years ago, Calumet was a big copper mining town. It's hard to believe that in 1900 there were over 60,000 people who lived here. Today, there is only about a thousand. And to this day, 2,000 miles of copper mines snake beneath the village and all around it. The mines have been closed since 1968, because it was thought that all of the copper had been mined, and because of a labor strike.

At least, that's what everyone was *told*.

Problem is, that wasn't the truth. The mines were really closed because of mysterious copper creatures. They thought if they closed the mines, the creatures would never surface.

And they were right—for a while. The creatures never returned. Very few people even knew about them. The copper creatures kept to themselves, in the mines, never seen by anyone.

Until this summer.

This summer, the copper creatures came out of hiding, and two kids in Calumet were the first to discover them.

Calvin and me.

2

Calvin returned from the garage with his hiking shoes.

"Let's go exploring," he said. Calvin has been on this kick to go 'exploring' in the woods. He likes to hike down a trail and then go off on his own to see what he can find.

Trouble is, being that he's only eight, he can't go alone. So, Mom usually makes me go with him. Sometimes it's fun, but other times its just plain boring. We never find much of anything. Oh, we see lots of animals: deer, raccoons, snakes, birds toads . . . things like that. But we never really find anything exciting. Once, Calvin found the skull of a deer. He took it home, cleaned it up, and put it on his dresser. It's still there today. Gross.

Speaking of today, I really wasn't interested in going for a hike. But two things changed my mind. One, I really couldn't think of anything better to do, and two, I knew that if I took Calvin exploring, he wouldn't get into trouble . . . which meant *I* wouldn't get into trouble.

"Where do you want to go?" I asked.

Calvin shrugged. "I don't care," he replied. "Anywhere different. Let's go somewhere we haven't been before."

"We could ride our bikes over to St. Louis Mine Road and find a trail that goes off into the woods," I suggested.

"Hey, that would be cool!" Calvin said. "That'll be the perfect place to do some exploring!"

It's also the perfect place to keep you from breaking any more windows, I thought. St. Louis Mine Road runs east out of town, and there's woods and fields on both sides. I've been out there many times before, but not Calvin. This would be a new place for him to explore, so I knew he'd be excited.

In no time at all we'd found our helmets, hopped onto our bikes, and were peddling down the block rounding onto 1st Street, which turns into St. Louis Mine Road.

"I wonder what we'll find?" Calvin asked as we peddled beneath a gray, overcast sky.

"You never know," I said.

We continued riding on the shoulder of the road. Calvin kept his eye out for anything he thought might be worth exploring.

Suddenly, he hit his brakes hard. Gravel crunched as his bike came to a halt. I stopped and turned around to look at him.

"What's the matter?" I asked.

Calvin was looking into the woods, and he raised his arm to point. "I saw something over there," he said.

"What did you see?" I asked.

"I don't know," he said. "But something moved."

"It was probably a deer," I replied.

"No, it wasn't a deer," Calvin said.

I stared for a moment, but all I could see were trees.

"Well, whatever it was, it's gone now," I said. "Come on . . . let's keep going."

"No," Calvin insisted. "Let's go see what it is."

I wasn't in the mood to argue, so I hopped off my bike and laid it in the brush just off the shoulder of the road. Calvin did the same. We took our helmets off and dropped them by our bikes.

"It was right over there," Calvin said. "Let's go find it."

Well, we found it, all right. And it certainly wasn't a deer. In fact, when we found out what it really was, I wished we'd never decided to go looking in the first place.

Once again, Calvin had managed to get himself—and *me*—into big trouble.

3

The brush was thick as we walked through the forest. Also: black flies were trying to eat us alive. They're tiny, biting flies that suck all of your blood. Well, not *all* of it, of course. But it seems like it. When those little buggers bite, they hurt. They were swarming all around us, landing on my neck and arms.

"Where is this thing?" I asked. I was beginning to doubt that Calvin saw anything at all. Like I said: it was probably just a deer or something. So far, though, I hadn't seen a thing. Not even a tiny bird.

"It's around here somewhere," Calvin said, looking all around. "It has to be."

"Whatever it was, it's long gone," I said.

"No, it's not," Calvin insisted. "I would've seen it."

We moved slowly through the brush. The swarm of black flies around my head was like a cloud, and I kept swatting my arm at them to keep them from landing at biting me. Calvin was doing the same thing.

Next time I'll wear bug spray, I thought.

"It was right around here where I saw it move," Calvin said. "It has to be here."

I guess if there was one good thing, Calvin was occupied . . . and he wasn't doing anything to get into trouble.

Unfortunately, trouble was only moments away.

"I'm just going to wait right here," I said, swishing the air to keep the black flies away. "Let me know when you find something."

Oh, Calvin found something, all right. No sooner had I spoke those words than something emerged from a brush pile. It emerged by standing on its hind legs and facing us.

And that something was a huge black bear!

4

Now, I don't know where *you* live, but where *we* live, we see black bears often. Oh, it's not like they wander into your yard or anything . . . although that does happen once in a while. Bears usually keep to themselves . . . like this one was doing.

But now the bear was standing on his hind legs, which meant that he felt threatened. If a bear feels threatened, watch out.

However, Calvin did the right thing: he yelled and clapped his hands, making lots of noise. The bear decided he didn't like it, dropped to all fours, and took off in the opposite direction, crashing through thick branches.

My heart was pounding. Bugs still swarmed my head, and I swatted at them.

"See?" Calvin said. "I told you I saw something!"

"Next time, let's get a better look before we go trudging into the woods," I said. "It's a good thing we didn't surprise that bear any more than we did. Otherwise, we might not have been so lucky."

"But that was cool, don't you think?" Calvin asked.

"Yes," I said, "it was cool. I just hope it doesn't happen again."

When we reached the shoulder of the road, we put our helmets back on, climbed back onto our bikes, and continued our journey. There was a thin two-track trail that I had seen before on an earlier ride. I'd heard that it was supposed to go way back into the woods, to an old ghost town. There wasn't supposed to be anything there anymore except old foundations and a few rotting structures that were falling down, but it would be neat to see. And Calvin would have a riot.

We pedaled until we saw the trail I was looking for. It went off to the left, to the north, and it was heavily overgrown with tall grass.

"Let's go that way," I said to Calvin.

"Where does it go?" Calvin asked as we slowed our bikes. We checked to make sure there were no cars coming, then we crossed the street.

"A ghost town," I replied.

"Awesome!" Calvin shouted. "Really?"

"That's what I hear," I said. "It's supposed to go to some town where miners used to live with their families. Years ago, when mines began shutting down, it was abandoned . . . and it turned into a ghost town."

"I've never been to a real ghost town before!" Calvin said as our bikes left the shoulder and merged onto the two-track.

"Neither have I," I said. "I bet it will be cool-looking . . . if we can find it."

Well, we would find it, all right. We would walk among the ruins, we would explore what was left of some very old buildings. We would even find an old penny with an Indian head on it.

But there was something else we would find.

Monsters.

Not monsters like you see on television or in comic books.

Real monsters.

Creatures that lived in the abandoned copper mines, all these years, waiting for the right time to emerge.

The time had come.

The copper creatures were coming back.

And for Calvin and me, it was the beginning of what was to be the scariest event of our lives . . . .

ABOUT THE AUTHOR

Johnathan Rand is the author of more than 50 books, with well over 2 million copies in print. Series include **AMERICAN CHILLERS, MICHIGAN CHILLERS, FREDDIE FERNORTNER, FEARLESS FIRST GRADER**, and **THE ADVENTURE CLUB.** He's also co-authored a novel for teens (with Christopher Knight) entitled **PANDEMIA.** When not traveling, Rand lives in northern Michigan with his wife and two dogs. He is also the only author in the world to have a store that sells only his works: **CHILLERMANIA!** is located in Indian River, Michigan. Johnathan Rand is not always at the store, but he has been known to drop by frequently. Find out more at:

www.americanchillers.com

JOIN THE FREE AMERICAN CHILLERS FAN CLUB!

It's easy to join . . . and best of all, it's FREE!
Find out more today by visiting:

WWW.AMERICANCHILLERS.COM

And don't forget to browse the on-line superstore, where you can order books, hats, shirts, and lots more cool stuff!